THINGS WE LOSE

AWP 10

THINGS WE LOSE

Stories by Roland Sodowsky

University of Missouri Press
Columbia

Copyright ©1989 by Roland Sodowsky
University of Missouri Press, Columbia, Missouri 65211
Printed and bound in the United States of America

Library of Congress Cataloging-in-Publication Data

Sodowsky, Roland
Things we lose / stories by Roland Sodowsky
p.   cm. — (AWP award series in short fiction)
ISBN 0-8262-0723-5 (alk. paper)
I. Title. II. Series: AWP (Series)
PS3569.0377T48 1989   89-4835
813'.54—dc20   CIP

∞™ This paper meets the minimum requirements of the American National
Standard for Permanence of Paper for Printed Library Materials, Z39.48, 1984.

Some of the stories in this collection originally appeared in the following
magazines: "Landlady," *Sou'wester*; "The Running Score," *Epoch*; and an earlier
version of "Witch" as "Witch on the Corner" in *Drumbeats Magazine* (Nigeria).

ACKNOWLEDGMENTS

Many thanks to Sul Ross State University, Yaddo, and the National Endowment for the
Arts for their support and aid. Special thanks to Edward Hower, Madelyn Alixopulos,
George and Willa Bartuska, Sue Doak, and Ernest Speck for their criticism and
suggestions.

FOR GARGI

The AWP Award Series in Short Fiction

This volume is the first-place winner of the annual AWP Award Series in Short Fiction, sponsored by the Associated Writing Programs, an organization of over ninety colleges and universities with strong curricular commitments to the teaching of creative writing, headquartered at Old Dominion University, Norfolk, Virginia.

Each year, a collection of outstanding short fiction is selected by a panel of distinguished fiction writers from among the many manuscripts submitted to the AWP Award Series competition. The University of Missouri Press is proud to be associated with the series and to present *Things We Lose* as the 1989 selection.

CONTENTS

LANDLADY

The ceiling fans on the screened veranda had not always been silent. For months, the housing on one had clacked around lazily as the blades whirled; the other had just two speeds, one too fast, the other too slow, and the regulators for both had buzzed steadily, irritatingly. So, armed with tools and coils of insulated wire, the *mbakara* had come home from the Project and dismantled the regulators and rewired them. Then he had the stepladder brought from the storage room, climbed up, and in ten minutes the housing was more securely fastened than when it came from the factory. The white-jacketed steward had watched him casually, without curiosity: for who can say what a *mbakara* will do? When he was finished, he had turned the fans on and watched and listened, nodding; the buzzing was gone, the housing stable, each fan had five graduated speeds.

"Bring me a drink, Ezekiel," he had said, and sat in a large wicker chair under the silent fans with a tight smile on his face. For he was a technical man, a technical man first; what, they all agreed at the club, even the Indigenous Director, the Continent would never have of its own: a technical man who was not afraid to step from the *Big Oga* seat of his Mercedes, elbow through the gawking, idled workers, and get his hands dirty; who could glance over a warehouse inventory sheet or a drainage layout and have fifty backs bending to in minutes, look into the guts of a diesel engine and restore power to a city by saying do this or do that; who, when a hard decision was necessary, would not remember some urgent business back in his home village and disappear, but would make it, make it and stand by it and not squirm and lie and accuse a subordinate of misunderstanding him.

A technical man first: generations of grim men who could make derricks suck oil out of the ocean, transform silt-filled rivers into deep-water harbors and rain forests into endless miles of rubber trees set in geometric patterns.

Or repair a noisy fan. He had sat in the silent breeze, and then it was that he had heard the madwoman for the first time, somewhere beyond the bare, clean-swept strip of ground behind the house, somewhere in the bush back there, scolding in that odd, cadenced voice, not angry but cross, *patiently* cross, he thought: like someone explaining and explaining what has been explained before and has to be explained again. He listened and peered,

1

and saw nothing, and it grew dark and the voice still came from the bush, somewhere in there among the mud huts and gleams of light from candles and kerosene lanterns and cooking fires. On and on. The steward called him to dinner, and afterwards he took his whisky on the veranda and listened again.

And again the next evening. He asked the steward, "What is that? Who's that talking?"

"Sah?"

"Who's that talking? That voice?"

"Sah?"

It was to the steward, he realized, as if he had asked, "What is that air?" As indistinguishable as one long banana leaf from another, as children's cries in a schoolyard.

When he understood, the steward explained without even a shrug, as though he were speaking of rain in the rainy season.

"She mad, sah. Madwoman."

"What's she saying?"

"Sah?"

"The madwoman. What does she say?"

He listened. "She say dey don take her land. Dis land her land."

"Who took it?"

He shrugged then. "*Dey,* sah. She say all dis land her land. Dey don take ahm."

A few evenings later he saw her. The gardener next door was breaking out a plot of land for planting, swinging a heavy-bladed, short-handled hoe, when the voice began, cross, insistent—*reasonable,* somehow, he thought, knowing she was in the right, assuming the gardener would eventually understand, would do what she wanted. Would leave. The *mbakara* listened, the fans rotating softly, the glass with the clear ice and the fresh quarter of lime cold in his hand, and then she was there, directly across the bare strip of ground, scolding the gardener, gesturing in cadence with her voice. The gardener glanced at her, went on with his digging. Her skin was the color of the freshly turned soil. She held a matchet in her right hand, the long blade thin from many sharpenings. She wore a sleeveless, collarless knit shirt, or undershirt perhaps it was, a lustreless maroon color, with a large tear on one side, and her lappa was the color of dead banana leaves. She was barefoot. Her headcloth was green, brighter than the palm fronds behind her, and tied in a stiff, slanting, high-crowned way that reminded him of those pictures of that Egyptian queen—what was her name? Her breasts swung gently as she shook her finger at the gardener.

The ice in the glass tinkled, and the steward said as he set down a fresh one, "She distahb you, sah?"

"Why should she disturb me?" Then he saw that she had moved a step closer to the veranda and was looking at him, talking to him, in that same steady, impatient voice.

"No, she is not disturbing me," he said.

The message was clear enough, he thought, even though he could not understand the words: *You have wronged me. In this way. And this. And also in this. Do you understand now? Why do you persist in not understanding?* Occasionally she broke off to turn and jab the end of the matchet into the ground, as if to resume the work, the life they, *he,* had interrupted. Then she straightened and began again.

He did not see her for a few days, and then she returned, standing in the same place next to the rotting stump of a matcheted pawpaw tree, the stump and the twiglike beginnings of a sapling beside it, just leafing, barely reaching her hip. She seemed more disturbed than before, and as she talked she edged closer to the veranda, jabbing the matchet hard into the clean-swept ground, until she was a few feet from the screen. He saw that she had the delicate features of the riverine peoples, those who centuries ago had floated in their black canoes down the river that curved southward out of the Bambuto Mountains, down to where the webbed delta area of mangrove swamps began, had settled and spread slowly inland and back up the river and become the landowners, the landlords to the tribes that followed. A small-seeming face, unlined, crisply symmetrical.

As she grew more agitated her voice rose a pitch higher, although her face remained calm, her lips did not contort in anger. She waved the matchet, not threateningly, he thought, but to punctuate, like a lecturer's pointer; her breasts lifted and fell, and once when her headcloth slipped he saw that her hair, like the market women's, was short and tied in half a dozen black twists. Her eyes never left his face.

"Ezekiel," he called. When the steward came, he said, "Tell her to go away."

The steward went out the side door of the veranda and spoke to her, gesturing toward the bush. She took a step backwards, but her eyes were still on the *mbakara* and her voice rose higher.

"Go!" the steward shouted in English, and again she stepped back, still talking. She retreated stubbornly, her voice rising steadily. At the far edge of the bare ground the steward suddenly picked up a palm branch and, before the *mbakara* realized what he intended, stripped its leaves and slashed at her twice, once across her arm and chest and again across her back as she turned.

"Ezekiel! Stop that." The *mbakara* swore. "That's enough. Finish. Get back in here."

Even then the woman continued to scold, not the steward but the *mbakara,* rubbing the welt on her arm, her face calm, the rhythms of her complaint undisturbed, irrefutable.

*   *   *

The hot months of the dry season passed, the rains began. Now as they
returned from the Project the driver, squinting over the wheel to avoid the
potholes and the treacherous taxis, would sometimes plunge the gray
Mercedes into a dark wall of water, a torrent, and just as suddenly come
out to the dry road again; or in the night, a single deafening crack of
thunder, and then the rain would roar on the corrugated metal roof for
hours. Soon, the *mbakara* knew, the hours would be days; the bills of
lading, letters, even manila folders in the office would be limp with
humidity; the steward would have to iron his clothes dry, and still they
would smell of dampness and rot, like the decaying undergrowth in the
bush.

*I will tell you once more of my wronging, and of the cause of this
wronging.*

She was there. She had not come close again since the steward had struck
her, but kept by the pawpaw stump and the new tree beside it, fully leafed
now and shoulder-high to her. She scolded him as he drank slowly, dully
listening; he had gotten used to her and her voice, like the women along
the highway with their staggering headloads of firewood or the small
ragged men pushing their black bicycles loaded with cassava roots up the
long hills.

He thought of other things, the threatened strike at the Project, the
exasperating disappearance of copper tubing, the letter—letters—he had
not written to his wife. He frowned; tonight he would write. Or this
weekend.

It is you who are to blame.

"Sssst!"

The *mbakara* started, then scowled; that voiceless call, irritating to all
foreigners; he had trained himself to ignore it. If a man wanted to talk to
him, let him speak, not hiss like a snake.

"Sssst!"

The madwoman stopped her scolding and turned. It was, the *mbakara*
saw, the gardener next door, standing among the yam hills he had shaped
on the plot of freshly broken land, his narrow face alert, mobile, smiling
broadly as he beckoned to her. She watched him without moving. He was
barefoot and shirtless, his tight black trousers rolled above his knees. The
evening sun glinted on his biceps and the smooth muscles of his chest. He
motioned to her to come closer, pointing to something in his other hand,
something hidden by the green yam foliage. She stepped toward him, then
stopped. He grinned, white teeth glistening, glanced admiringly at the
thing concealed by the leaves, beckoned. When she did not move, he held
up a brassiere —black, gauzy, light as a spider's web, not at all like the bulky
things the market women wore. The *mbakara* chuckled softly; almost

certainly, the gardener had pilfered it from the young wife of his master, the engineer who lived next door and who had gone home on leave.

As the madwoman started toward the gardener, he backed away, matching her step for step, grinning, waving the bit of cloth. He backed out of the yam hills and moved slowly toward the doorway of his quarters, a little one-room house of concrete blocks with a single screenless window, stopping when she stopped and holding the prize out invitingly to her. Reaching the doorway, he stepped inside, never taking his eyes from her; he held the bra out with both hands, beamed, shook his head in wonder, fitted it against his chest. She came steadily toward him, and as she passed through the doorway he kept the bra just out of her grasp. The door closed, the *mbakara* heard the wooden bar being dropped, and then the gardener closed the shutter of the window.

After dinner the *mbakara* returned to sit with his whisky on the dark veranda. The security lights had been turned on around the house, illuminating the yam mounds, the young pawpaw tree and the stump, the door of the gardener's quarters. The *mbakara* thought of the madwoman, grown silent as she succumbed to the gardener's strategy. The smoothly functioning mechanics of the transaction, the gardener's perception of the barter value of the stolen or perhaps discarded garment, of what he could do—distract with a wisp of foreign nonsense a madwoman from her madness, trick her vanity or petty acquisitiveness into overruling her obsession, into closing her mouth and opening her thighs—pleased, appealed to the *mbakara*. Sweating in the heavy night air, he watched the gardener's door, even strained to listen; he recalled the workers' quarters he had inspected at the Project, houses like the gardener's: a bench, a wooden chair and small square table, a bed without mattress or springs, or a mat on the floor, a piece of coarse cloth for cover. Her eyes, he wondered . . . lappa tossed over the chair, headcloth tumbled away by the grinning, eager gardener . . . would her eyes be fixed on the prize, the bit of cloth?

He drank his whisky and called the steward to bring another, and later still another before he sent him home. The night watchmen, armed with slingshots and stout *iroko* clubs, said "Good evening, sah" to his silhouette on the veranda, and returned to the front porch to sleep on their mats. The breeze from the silently turning fans kept away the mosquitoes that slipped through the mesh. He finished his drink and stretched, settling back in the chair, and was just dozing off when he heard the voice of the madwoman, muted but scolding as usual, and the gardener's grunting reply as the door opened.

There was a flicker of a candle from inside. The woman stood in the doorway: *Here is how you have wronged me. In this way, and this.* She jabbed her matchet against the door. *And also in this. Do you understand? Why—*

"Ennhh! Finish! Go now!" the man said. His hand flashed into the light of the doorway, and she stumbled backwards but did not fall, barely interrupting the rhythm of her complaint. The door slammed, but she stood her ground: *And in this. And this also. Must I explain it to you again?*

The *mbakara* lifted his glass, found it empty. He went in to the bar, refilled it, and returned to drink and listen and watch the woman. At last she turned from the door and walked along the edge of the bush, scolding, occasionally slashing at the ground with the matchet.

*   *   *

When the rainy season came in earnest, the *mbakara* began to think of his annual leave. Eleven weeks, ten weeks it was now. He thought of the things he would do: repairs to be made on the house, investments to be made from the account fattened each month by his stateside paychecks, possibly a vacation trip somewhere. And he thought of his wife, vaguely, irritably; he could not associate the attractive woman in the large framed photograph on his bedroom dresser with the fragments of remembrances, images in his mind: filtered sunlight on her as she opened the drapes in the den; the jangle of the telephone and her assured warmth as she accepted an invitation to someone's house; their immaculate bedroom and her somewhere in it doing something, always something that was somehow done without disturbing, displacing anything; Sunday mornings, coffee with her on the patio, talk of—what? The poodle racing wildly about the fenced yard, the patch of grass that was never quite green? Something. The poodle brushing against the hem of her gray robe.

Home leave. It irritated him that he felt no compelling need to go home such as one could hear in the voice or read in the eyes of the men, especially the younger ones, at the club. He had only a vague desire not to stay: the lushness of this place sometimes oppressed him, disturbed, like his over-sized house, its walls bristling with air conditioners, his sense of function. Wet vegetation crept over the swept ground around the house; he could feel mold, smoothly alive, on his shoes as he tied them in the morning; the new pawpaw tree now stood eight, nine feet high, clusters of fruit already forming.

The madwoman had discarded her torn knit top and replaced it with the gardener's barter. When she appeared to scold the *mbakara* in the morning, protected by a large piece of green banana leaf if it was raining, she wore her lappa tucked at her waist and stood by the new pawpaw tree in her odd combination of native cloth and the product of western engineering and chemistry and notions of displaying the female body, jabbing the wet soil and berating the *mbakara* for his part in her disenfranchisement. Later, when the sun burned overhead and the steam rose from the bush, she wrapped the lappa tightly over her breasts.

On a Saturday afternoon, the rain falling steadily, the *mbakara* left his papers scattered the length of the dining table and went to the veranda. By the chair was a letter from his wife, opened but unread since the day before. He read it slowly, stopping to watch a fat-bodied bird with a long beak dart from the new pawpaw tree to snatch food from the clouds of insects above the strip of bare ground; he read of bridge afternoons, a plumber's bill, children's grade reports, a brunch, a luncheon, while a lizard scampered noisily on the metal roof of the veranda and the rain whispered, and then the madwoman, a battered porcelain basin balanced on her head, appeared at the edge of the bush, talking to him.

With her matchet she cut two banana leaves and wedged them in the branches to keep the rain off; she tugged at another banana leaf and braced up its flappy sides with sticks so that it curved in a long vee down to her feet; a rivulet of clear water soon ran from its tip, and she set the basin to catch the water. She began to wash a small pile of clothing, using a piece of the yellow soap that the women sold in long unwrapped bars in the market. She stood as she washed, bending from the waist, but now and then she straightened to look at him as she talked: *this land, you see, is mine; it is not your land; you are here wrongfully on this land, for first some mbakara like you took it from me and then they gave it to black men and now the black men have given it to you, so it is not right that you are here.* The word *mbakara* he could clearly understand as she talked, for it was shouted at him by the children along the crowded streets every day as he was driven to and from the Project; everything else he felt he understood: the logic, the . . . balance? . . . yes, like lifters in an engine, the balance of her arguments, *what is* against *what is not,* as he heard it in the rise and fall of her voice.

When she had finished, she cut another banana leaf to broaden her shelter and draped the clothing on the dead limbs beneath it. Then she took off the bra and unwrapped her headcloth, washed them, and hung them to dry, carefully smoothing out the creases in the headcloth. Her heavy breasts lifting and swaying, lighter in color than the sodden earth, she adjusted the vee-shaped leaf so that the rivulet was shoulder-high. As she talked to the *mbakara* in her measured, impatient rhythms, she opened her lappa and removed it, folded it neatly, and then stepped beneath the trickle of water, flinching as it struck her, shifting her shoulders and arching, then bending, turning to wet her chest and stomach; she interrupted herself only when the water struck her face. She stepped back under the shelter to soap herself, using the piece of soap frugally, making a small triangle of lather in her pubic hair, replacing the soap on its scrap of paper, working the lather with her fingers, now her knuckles, over her stomach and breasts to her underarms. Her intent scrubbing somehow reminded the *mbakara* of the way she jabbed the matchet into the soil. He watched the madwoman, the full rounds of her belly and buttocks, her sturdy thighs and arms, and thought again of his wife—of shimmering emerald or silver or ruby liquids in gracefully curved bottles in her bathroom, of the shrill hum of her hair dryer, the mingled odor of scents and heat from electric coils as she opened the bathroom door and came out in her gray robe. He remembered their utility room—the intricate array of lights and switches on the washer, the low roar of the dryer, the thick discs of glass in the doors of the machines.

When she had rinsed away the soap, the mad woman patted herself dry with a scrap of cloth, shook out the lappa vigorously, and wrapped herself in it again, tucking the loose end tightly under her left arm. With a quick stroke she slashed the vee-shaped banana leaf and, holding the severed piece over her head, came to stand by the new pawpaw tree and scold the *mbakara*. As he studied the smoothness of her face, the fineness of detail of cheekbones and brow, her heavy lips and large, wide-set eyes, he wondered what she saw of him through the mesh in the darker shadow of the veranda—khaki shorts, the whiteness of his legs perhaps and of his face and neck above his chest, matted, unlike the gardener's, with thick brown hair, beginning to gray? Always her eyes seemed fastened on his as she spoke: *Since you do not belong here, it is only right that you leave; I have explained this to you before; you must leave, for I must plant yams here, and cassava and pumpkins.*

She dropped the leaf and pierced it with the matchet, without anger, the *mbakara* thought, but simply to show that she was ready to begin her work. The rain, he realized, had stopped; the gray overcast was breaking up, the sun glinting through. He called the steward to rouse the dozing driver to take him to the club.

Late that night he awoke and could not sleep again. He lay on the broad bed under the sheet listening to the air conditioner, watching the thin gleams from the security lights outside. He switched on the bedside lamp and then turned it off to shut out the starkness of the large room, the bare walls, the dresser with the single framed photograph on it. Irritated by the whine of the air conditioner, he got up and made his way to the veranda, wearing only his briefs, and when he opened the veranda door, he heard her: *There is no question about this. You know I have been wronged, you are part of this wronging. You must make it right. It is far too long now that you have not made it right. Where are my yams that should be leafing from this soil, in this season of new rains? Where is the waterleaf? Tell me where.*

Her eyes, her teeth flashed white in the glare of the security lights. She loosened her lappa, adjusted it, tucked in the edge as she talked. Standing close to the screen, he glanced at the gardener's dark little house, at the bush where no lights shone, heard a single heavy drum far off, somewhere beyond the hills of oil palm trees. He listened to the woman, remembering her bathing under the clear rivulet of rainwater, and then he went into the house, took from the storage room three—no, he thought, four—large bars of soap packaged in gold foil, returned to the veranda, and opened the screen door.

"Sssst! Come," he said. She watched him silently.

"Come. Come here." He held out one of the glittering bars. "These are for you. Come here."

As she came slowly closer, he realized in surprise how short she was; no more than five feet, he thought, or even less. She shifted the matchet to her left hand and took the gold bar, turned it this way and that, then looked at him, waiting.

"Soap," he said. "Good soap." Taking the bar from her and opening the foil, he held it for her to smell, then made lathering motions over his chest and stomach. He pressed it into her hand and held out the other bars.

"All for you," he said, and motioned toward the door. "Come." He put his hand on her shoulder and pushed her inside.

In the bedroom she stood dumbly, blinking in the sudden bright light. He took the soap from her and put it with the other bars on the dresser, gesturing and saying again, "for you," while she watched him. A white man, he thought, taking the matchet from her and laying it on the floor; a *mbakara*, sweat, hairy chest and all; her first good look. He pulled the tuck of the lappa and opened it, drew it away and tossed it over a chair. But when he pushed her toward the bed, she resisted, turning from him and picking up the lappa to fold it as she had done that afternoon. He kept his hands on her, and when she had finished, urged her toward the bed, pushing her onto it. As he switched the light out, he saw that she was fearfully testing the strange resilience of the bed, putting her weight on one knee, then the other, watching the mattress sink and rise. He smiled then, thinking: and your first real bed. A pulsing exaltation surged through him, a need to master, and he found her quickly in the darkness and covered her.

*   *   *

He awoke with a start. Morning? No, the security light still glinted on the ceiling over the top of the heavy drape. She was sleeping, curled close to him for warmth, the sheet and blanket pulled in tight against her. He found her breast and lifted it, felt the thick nipple, then thought: No. They'll be up, all over . . . the gardener, houseboys out. He switched on the light and shook her shoulder, and when she sat up sleepily, handed her the lappa, motioning that she put it on. When she had finished, her eyes dumbly inspecting him, he put the bars of soap and the matchet in her arms, turned off the light, led her to the veranda, urged her down the steps, saying "Go. Go now," and locked the door behind her.

As he recrossed the veranda, she began once more: *Mbakara, I ask you, where are the yams that should be leafing here? Where are—*

*   *   *

The *mbakara* bought a parasol in midweek, returning with it wrapped in
a sheet of newspaper to where the driver waited in the Mercedes. And on
Friday, coming home from the Project, he again plunged into the muddy,
reeking labyrinth of the market and came out with bags containing a large
bath towel printed with pink and purple and yellow flowers, a pair of green
plastic sandals, underclothing in iridescent colors, a filmy American-made
blouse, pink with red buttons and an enormous flounce, and a headcloth
of some heavy synthetic material, brilliantly orange. He locked the bags
carefully in his steamer trunk, having no desire for the flapping tongues of
the steward and night watchmen and driver to carry the story of his
purchases back to the Project.

He now took his evening drink in the living room, slumped in one of the
blocky overstuffed chairs where he could not see or hear the madwoman.
Only after the steward had left, the faint lights had gone out in the bush,
the night watchmen had made their sleepy circuit, did he appear on the
veranda.

He began to write to his wife regularly. Sitting nearly every evening
in the living room with a yellow legal pad on his lap, he described for
the first time the trees along the narrow, crowded streets loaded with
enormous calabash fruits, avocados, mangos, and green oranges; the
women who squatted along the road selling cigarettes one at a time from
gold-foiled Benson and Hedges packets, selling curled and blackened
smoked fish impaled on long sticks, selling ogusi seeds and peanuts
("Groundnuts they call them here; makes more sense, doesn't it?")
measured out in little milk glass jars and wrapped in cones of paper torn
from used cement bags, selling strings of snails each larger than a child's
head and mounds of wet, black periwinkles shaped like thimble-sized
Christmas trees, tiny piles of dried crayfish and slices of cooked goat
meat cut skin and all from a fly-covered haunch while buyer and seller
haggled over the size. He even told her of the leper who had pressed his
face, like melted plastic, against the window of the car one day, and of
the thing, the head and trunk of a man, a madman, he had seen half a
year earlier rotting in the marketplace.

He described the problems at the Project, his frustration at having to hire
"brothers" from the huge extended family of the Indigenous Director,
typists who couldn't type, file clerks who stole reams of photocopying
paper and resold them in the market, laborers who made cement blocks by
day and stole them by night. He wrote about the breakdowns that allowed
dozens of workers to chat or snooze in the shade until he and his grim,
swearing, sweating crew of technical people found a solution—had a
replacement for a burnt-out bearing flown in from Lagos or Frankfurt or
Liverpool, welded a brace under a tottering storage tank, sorted out the

crackling wires at a substation struck by a fool, killed of course, driving a bulldozer.

Sometimes, when the steward's clatter of dishes annoyed him, he went to the veranda. The madwoman was almost always there these days, waiting to begin her lecture, he thought, or maybe rehearsing it. He listened to her with contentment; he might call her in later, might not. He had taken to setting his alarm clock to go off well before daylight, before the night watchmen stirred and the driver and steward came from their quarters, chewsticks in their mouths, to urinate at the edge of the bush. It amused him that the alarm never awakened the woman; it was to her, he thought, an alien, meaningless sound, indistinguishable from the air conditioners. On Saturday nights, when he knew the steward would not appear the next day until time to prepare lunch, he was tempted not to set the alarm; he liked the woman's warmth against him, liked to stroke the strong smoothness of her thigh when he half-awakened in the darkness and dozed off again. But he thought better of it.

It is wrong that these strange houses of yours are here, with their metal roofs and machines that make strange noises; remove them. My father and his wives, my mother among them, and their fathers before them, build good houses here; they build houses of poles stripped of their bark and set in the ground with pliant branches woven skillfully among them, wove them together and then dug a hole here—do you see where I show you?—dug a hole here and found the proper clay and the women packed it carefully around the woven branches and the poles to form strong cool walls, and the boys cut the mats, many hundreds of mats, from the proper trees to make a strong cool roof, and now you have destroyed all of this. The women put a leafy green twig in the wet clay of the new walls and when the twig died the walls were dry and the house was ready for life, and now you have destroyed all of this.

It amused him to take the lappa away and find her wearing the lavender or mint-green or bright yellow wisps of underclothing he had doled out to her. He began showing her things in the house, not to satisfy her curiosity, for she seemed to have none, seemed only to stare dumbly at him, at the thick graying hair of his chest, the whiteness of his upper thighs, the brown hair of his arms and legs. In the bathroom, he put her hand against the stubble of his face, then switched on the small black machine in his hand, shaved the place she had touched, and made her touch it again. He made her hold one end of the shaver's coiled cord, then pulled it out straight and released it. He put her hand under the tap, watching her incomprehension as the water became warm, chuckling as she jerked away when it was hot. He took her to the kitchen, being sure that the curtains were tightly drawn before he turned on the lights, and showed her the stove, pointing to a burner where blue flames suddenly appeared, disappeared. He opened the freezer and made her touch the frost-coated side, smiling again as she flinched and shivered; he made her hold a frozen chicken, smell the stone-hard flesh. In the living room, she muttered some low sound of fear and clutched at him as she felt the thick carpet yield under her feet. He forced her to feel it, touch it with her hands, and then, aroused by her fear and uncertainty, he powerfully pushed her struggling down on the strange synthetic fur.

He thought of his leave more often—eight weeks, seven, six—and discussed plans, projects in his letters to his wife: a new sprinkler system for the lawn, a gas line to the outdoor grill; a trip to—where? Somewhere, anywhere. His son had taken an unexpected interest in computers, his wife had written, and this pleased him; he wrote of systems, of applications, the limitless possibilities.

The Project, he wrote, would be the first of such magnitude ever completed on schedule in the country, without requiring additional money at a critical point; the Company was sure to be offered new contracts, and he would be in an enviable position, for the Government would insist that he have a hand in all new projects. He could name his own terms; he might even quit and become a consultant, spend a few days here, a few there for staggering fees, return home. The Indigenous Director was a powerful man and, with a little encouragement, would see to it that he was called often. . . .

When he went into the market now to buy earrings with bits of colored glass in them, gold-colored bangles, and small boxes of talcum for the mad woman, he also bought gifts for his wife—lengths of heavy cotton splashed in tie-dye patterns, woven raffia mats, carved ebony figures, batiks, bronze heads of ancient rulers from Benin, grotesque little carved stools, huge ceremonial masks.

The mad woman now came to the veranda door quickly when he opened it. Sometimes, when he awoke in the night but had no wish to bring her in, he quietly opened the jalousies to the veranda and, hidden by the curtains, listened to her: *It is long past the time when you should have left; take away these machines that make strange noises in the night; the night should be silent; take away these machines that carry you quickly from place to place and make the dust to fill the air in the dry season; a man has feet, a man should walk slowly when he must go to some other place, and not fill the air with dust in the dry season. Mbakara, go now. Why do you not go now?* He listened, and felt a certain contentment, and it did not occur to him to wonder why he felt this way, just as he did not wonder that to the rise and fall of her voice he now supplied meaning, or that, though he supplied it, it did not touch him; less than a woman's fluttering, ineffectually arresting hand was her constant injunction to him to go. He listened, and returned to bed, and occasionally he would think of his wife in the soft, directed flow of her bedside lamp, adjusting as she turned the pages of her novel her reading glasses, moving the ivory bookmark he had brought from somewhere. But more often he thought of the woman standing outside by the new pawpaw tree, of the whiteness of her strong even teeth, the brown heat of her breasts and their darker centers, the warmth as he traced the straight path of her spine and the sudden sweep of her buttocks while she slept. Sometimes when he thought of her in this way, he rose again and brought her in.

One night, when less than a month remained before his home leave, he walked through the darkened house and opened the jalousies to hear her, but there was no sound, no movement along the strip of bare ground or in the edge of the bush beyond it. The *mbakara* peered at the shadows where he imagined there might be openings into the bush, but saw nothing. He unlocked the door to the veranda, walked to the screen, and waited expectantly, for on the rare occasions when she had not been there already, talking, the sound of the lock, or the appearance of his silhouette on the veranda, he was not sure which, had produced her quickly. But she did not come. From somewhere toward the center of the city he heard music, not the intricate patterns of native drums but the steady amplified beat of electronic instruments. It began to rain, although lower in the sky over the oil palms he could see a handful of stars.

He waited, but saw nothing, heard only the rain falling. He waited, his eyes searching the bush for flickers of light, but there was nothing. He went back to the bedroom and took a pair of earrings from his steamer trunk, ignoring the unreasonableness of the idea that, if his presence had not lured the mad woman forth, the earrings would. At the outside veranda door, turning the earrings so that they flashed in the light, he said "Come" once, and then again, before the absurdity of it—a *mbakara* in his briefs holding out a pair of earrings and calling to the rain, apparently, in the middle of the night—silenced him.

The rain's tempo increased and then abruptly stopped. He listened once more, squinting at the shadows in the bush, and turned to go in.

Then he heard her.

And in this way also have I been wronged; I will tell you—

"Ennhh! Go! Go now!"

The gardener's hand flashing in the light of his doorway, the madwoman stumbling backwards—the *mbakara* had seen it all before, but had felt nothing, nothing like the coldness gathering inside him. She stumbled, but this time, encumbered by the matchet in her right hand, the parasol and something else in her left, some small thing, she fell heavily in the wet grass as the gardener's door slammed, her flame-orange headcloth tilting, her voice rising sharply. She got up quickly, shouting *Yes! I will tell you of this wronging!* She raised the matchet and brought it down hard against the door, embedding the end of the blade, wrenched it out and struck again, leaving the knife quivering in the door while she adjusted her headcloth.

Tell you of it very simply—

She opened the parasol, although the rain had stopped, raised it, and then worked the matchet loose from the door. *When the first mbakara came to this place, my land, they brought machines—*

Cold he felt momentarily in the hot wet night, and then the hot anger flashing through him like the flash of the matchet, of the flame-colored headcloth.

In that concrete shack, he thought; that grinning little bastard.

—brought machines and the machines of the mbakara pushed the trees and the yam plots from this place—

Something in his hand, like dried peas: he looked at the earrings, grimaced, and opened the veranda door to fling them out, then stopped. She was moving toward the veranda.

—pushed me and the trees and the yam plot from it.

She stood by the new pawpaw tree, her bangles flashing on her wrists, headcloth towering and glinting in the security lights, holding her parasol over her. Something that looked like wadded brown paper was stuffed under the edge of her lappa, between her breasts.

The mbakara built these strange houses—

As she talked she bent and struck the ground with her matchet from this, then that angle, cutting wedges from the wet soil.

—these houses that are not of stripped branches—

He glanced at the gardener's quarters, saw that it was dark, then held out the earrings in the palm of his hand.

"Come," he said. Birdseed, he thought as he shook the earrings in his hand. Crumbs. As she moved from the pawpaw tree to him, he felt the pure heat of his increasing anger and smiled.

—are not of stripped branches and the clay of this earth—

"Come," he said, taking the parasol from her and closing it, putting it back in her hand and pushing her up the veranda steps. Her plastic sandals flapped as she walked ahead of him to the bedroom.

—are not roofed with the proper mats, which should not be built here.

After he had shut the bedroom door behind her and turned on the light, she opened the parasol again and held it up, as if to shield herself from the bright bulbs.

Then the new black men came, and the mbakara gave these strange houses that should not be here to the new—

The *mbakara* held out the earrings. "Look. For you." He twisted the matchet from her hand, laid it on the floor, and placed the earrings in her palm, but when her fingers did not close upon them and she continued talking, he took them again and held them to her ears. "For you. Take them now." He smiled again. "Bonus night. Take them." He pressed their sharp edges against her ears, watching her face, but she turned her head away without changing expression.

—gave them to the new black men, and those mbakara went away. And the new black men lived in these strange houses that were wrongfully built on my land.

"All right, all right now," the *mbakara* said. When he turned to put the earrings on the dresser, she stooped and retrieved the matchet. He pulled at the tuck of her lappa. As it came away, the wad of brown paper fell from her breasts to the floor, opened, and peanuts rolled and scattered around their feet.

They lived in the houses and would not return my land to me, although they were black men.

For a moment, he could not comprehend the meaning of them; the shelled peanuts rolled away in every direction while he stood holding the corner of the lappa, and then he understood. He dropped the lappa. *They lived in the houses for a few seasons—*

"Peanuts," he said. "Peanuts he gave you." He slapped her, the sound sharp even over the air conditioner, bending her over and turning her sideways to him, the headcloth tumbling away. "Ten kobo worth of peanuts, God damn you!" He brought the open palm of his other hand up and caught her full in the face, knocking her back against the wall, and stepped forward to hit her again, the wetness of her saliva and the impact of her flesh rich and sweet in his hands, but she swung blindly with the matchet and he barely dodged out of the way.

—for a few seasons, and there were no yam plots for me, no frames of bent sticks for the long pumpkins to grow large on. Her voice high and wavering, she stood erect again, blood dribbling from her nose over her mouth and chin.

"Shut up, shut up now. No more talk." Remembering the night watchmen asleep on their mats on the front porch and fearing that she might be heard even over the noise of the air conditioners, the *mbakara* tried to put his hand over her mouth, but she backed away, gripping the rough wooden handle of the matchet and raising the blade. Setting the open parasol on the floor, she stooped to retrieve her headcloth without taking her eyes from him, settled it on her head, and then took up the parasol again.

No place for the waterleaf, and the bitterleaf, and the small peppers to grow—

The impatience and crossness in her voice increased, its pitch, the *mbakara* thought, going ever higher. He could not, for the moment, make out what to do, what to do quickly; the feel of her, skin and soft flesh beneath the skin, and bone and teeth, was still in his hands, and he felt, remembered, an exultation, a freedom in the hitting of her, and he wanted to do it again; the peanuts crunched under his feet and he remembered the gardener, stared at the iridescent bit of cloth tapering down to her crotch, its wetness, and thought, *from him,* and anger shot through him again, his hands raised, tightened into fists. But he thought of the night watchmen and dropped his hands to his sides.

The black men would not give my land back to me, and then the new mbakara came, the new mbakara, you among them—

She kept the parasol over the regal folds of her headcloth. She regained her composure, except that her voice quavered higher. Her eyes held his as she talked, and as always the reasonableness, the balance of what she had to say pleased him, appealed to him. He listened to her, let his anger drain away as her brown African eyes held him. He thought of other nights, and he regretted the swelling of her lip, the blood not yet dried under her nostrils. He remembered with a sudden rush of tenderness the acquiescence of her in their silent threshing on the bed, the comfort of her sleeping close to him, and a warmth as pure as his earlier anger flowed through him; he smiled and moved quickly to her, opening his arms to pull her to him, but she twisted away and simultaneously he saw the effortless movement of her wrist, the flat blurred arc of the matchet, and a long straight colorless line across his thigh, thin as a hair, an instant later red with blood, and then he felt the pain.

"Damn you!" He leaped back, stumbling against the bed, then regained his footing. Her voice was high now, strong in her anger: *the black men would not give my land back to me, and then the new mbakara came, the new mbakara, you among them, and the black men gave the new mbakara this land, my land, with the strange houses that should not be built here, gave it to the new mbakara—*

"All right, damn you!" The blood was pouring from the cut, already spotting the floor. He grabbed the lappa and flung it in her face. "All right, go! Go now!" He pointed at the door, but the lappa dropped and she stepped over it, the parasol still poised, and stood in the center of the room. *And now they are here, and you are here as wrongfully as the other mbakara and the black men who came after them. Why do you persist in remaining here when I tell you of these things?*

"Go now!" he hissed, mindful of the night watchmen. He stepped toward her but stopped when he saw the matchet blade draw back. "God damn you," he whispered, nearly sobbing. "Go! Get out!" But her voice rose steadily, and she did not move. The wetness down his leg frightened and infuriated him, and his hands began to shake.

You understand now the wrong that has been done to me; you understand now what must be done to undo this wrong; you must leave.

He went into the bathroom, pulled the coiled cord from the shaver, and stretched it, testing it, his hands quivering. Then he went back into the bedroom and began moving around her, taking a step, stopping, another step, the black cord doubled and concealed in his fists at his waist.

You must leave now, with your machines that go too quickly from place to place, which disturb the night. You must leave, and the other mbakara

with you, and you must not send other mbakara or other black men to this
place, for this is not their place.

She turned slowly as he moved, but he circled to her right so that the arc
of the matchet would be away from him, gradually closing on her, and when
he was within arm's reach he stepped forward quickly and put the cord over
her head and jerked, snapping her neck back and knocking the headcloth
away. He drove his knee into her lower back, and as she dropped the parasol
and fell he spun and fell with her, pinning her beneath him, driving his
forehead into the black twists of her hair and grinding her face into the
metal braces of the parasol. The matchet blade struck weakly over his leg,
but he kept the cord taut and buried in the softness of her throat and shifted
so that both knees were on her back, his leg beyond the matchet's reach,
and soon the matchet clattered on the floor and her writhing ceased.

He watched the clock by the bed: two minutes, three. Four. Five. He
pulled the cord from her, stood up, and went into the bathroom. There
were new, shallower cuts on his lower leg, and blood seeped steadily from
his thigh. He bathed the cuts, dried them, and poured on antiseptic,
groaning as he opened the long cut.

When he had stopped the bleeding and dressed the deeper wound, he took
a basin of soapy water and retraced his steps, washing up the trail of drying
blood as best he could. With his foot he turned the woman over on her back,
noting the angular marks the parasol braces had left on her face. He closed
the parasol and laid it by her side, refolded the lappa, and stood with it in
his hands, thinking of new contracts, consultancies, of what to do with the
body at his feet. He remembered the thing he had seen at the crossroads in
the marketplace, the madman, his legs and arms gnawed and torn away by
dogs and God knows what else in the night. A madman. She was mad: no
one, not her family, not the other squatters there in the bush, not the police,
not even a beggar, would touch her. He opened the lappa and rolled the
matchet, the parasol, and her sandals in it, then went to the living room and
looked cautiously through the curtains: the watchmen were asleep, curled
tightly in their thin blankets. the rain was falling again. He opened the door
to the veranda and unlocked the outside veranda door, then returned to the
bedroom and took a flashlight from a dresser drawer. Kneeling, he hoisted
her over his shoulder, grunting at the unexpected weight; he snugged the
rolled lappa under his arm and carried her to the veranda, where he stopped
and peered about intently; there was no light, no sound but the drumming
of the rain on the metal roof. He walked quickly over the bare wet ground
past the new pawpaw tree, and after several false starts found the opening
into the bush. Flinching away from the wet branches, he went in carefully
a few steps before switching on the light, keeping the beam down on the
narrow path. Mindful of things he had heard about but not seen—cobras,
even more deadly green mambas dangling from the tree limbs—he followed
the erratic patch for twenty-five, perhaps fifty yards, shivering in the rain,

and then he dropped the rolled lappa in a clump of tall green grass by the path and laid her awkwardly over it, face up. He held the light briefly on her face, already wet from the rain, the eyes wide and staring, her lips drawn back from her white, even teeth; then he hurried back along the path and across the cleared ground into the house.

* * *

Two evenings later, as he sat on the veranda, the brown vultures were circling thickly over the bush.

"Dis madwoman dead, sah," the steward said as he set the *mbakara's* drink down.

"What?" A squeak, barely discernible, was beginning in one of the overhead fans. He frowned. A bit of oil there.

"Madwoman, sah." The steward pointed toward the bush, the vultures. "In dah. She dead."

"How did she die?" Like all wounds in the tropics, his had become infected quickly, but the doctor at the Project had opened it and cleansed it thoroughly and given him antibiotics and a booster shot for tetanus, and now he rested his bandaged leg stiffly on a footstool.

The steward looked at him, perplexed. Who can tell what question a mbakara will ask? "She mad, sah. She dead." He padded back to the kitchen.

Home leave. Less than four weeks now. The *mbakara* thought of his wife's dry floral arrangements in asymmetrical, imperfectly blown glass vases, found in an antique shop somewhere . . . Vermont? New Hampshire, maybe. He smiled as he imagined her vaguely irritated, vaguely amused protestations when they unpacked the crate, the huge, grinning, triple-faced masks topped with white crocodiles and pink-spotted snakes, the reliefs of toad-shaped men squatting with club-like erections, of women with swollen bellies and navels like bananas and breasts like pawpaws. . . .

"But what . . . what do you expect me to *do* with these monstrosities?" she would say.

He smiled and sipped his drink, shook the quarter of fresh lime down into the ice. The new pawpaw tree was as high, no, higher now than the metal gable of the house, and a second tier of fruit was forming below the first, yellowing to ripeness. He stretched, grimaced at the pain in his thigh, and thought of the madwoman bathing her brown body with the yellow soap under the broad green banana leaf, bedecking herself with the gold-colored bangles and pink blouse and wisps of underclothing, thought of the rhythmic, patient reasonableness of her complaint as she stood under the rainbow-tinted parasol, remembered with a stab of regret the quiet, close warmth of her sleep and the quiet, close struggle of her dying, and then the *mbakara,* master through and through, frowned and put her from his mind.

SQUASHGIRL

The duplex was made of concrete blocks, long and narrow, with a corrugated metal roof. An almond tree shaded my front porch; nearby was a pawpaw with a tier of fat green fruit.

"My own food supply," I said to Freddie Campbell.

"Soak that rubbish in Milton for half an hour at least," he replied.

Burglar bars over the windows. The legs of the dining table stood in small rusty tins which Freddie said I was to fill with kerosene to discourage ants. The fridge sagged tiredly against the wall, its rear legs rusted through. A gas ring was missing from the cooker; the kitchen counter had rotted, the walls were filthy. Geckos, white and nearly transparent, watched me from the ceiling, and brown, surly cockroaches backed under the fridge when I passed by.

But mine own.

The other half of the house was vacant. I had thought to put the Beetle in the narrow driveway separating the next house from mine, but when I returned late in the afternoon a large Toyota was parked there.

Sitting in the shaded drive, my new neighbors watched me carry in my typewriter, books, clothing, and bedding: a stout woman of about twenty-five on the kitchen doorstep who tugged her lappa up over her breasts; a thin and bent old woman beside her who didn't bother; four naked boys, their heads clean-shaven, the eldest no more than six, who pointed at me and chorused "*Mbakara, mbakara!*" The younger woman was clearly in command; her voice, like ball bearings turning, rang with authority. Occasionally she shouted "Edett!" and a young man, lappa tied at his waist, poked his head out the kitchen door, answering "Sister!" When she called "Gloria!" a pinch-faced girl of about ten wrestled a wooden mortar outside to pound yams.

The boys marched in a circle, beating on Nido cans with sticks. Another girl, older, wearing a school uniform—blouse, wool skirt, knee socks, oxfords, tam—entered the house through the front door. A stocky, awkward, sullen-looking girl. As the day's heat eased, the man called Edett opened the curtains—yellow, with angle-jointed, sticklike brown figures cavorting on them—in the dining room. He too watched me, smiling.

When the equatorial night dropped on us, they went inside. Slapping at mosquitoes, I ate mackerel from the tin with dry bread. The smells of pounded yam, bitterleaf, and pepper soup drifted across from their dining table, which was opposite mine. Our kitchen doors and windows, bedroom windows, and the latticed walls of the clothes-drying areas faced each other. The houseboy, Edett (steward, as Freddie said we were to call them), and the girl, Gloria, ate on the kitchen step, but she was called in before she had finished. As I closed my kitchen door, Edett grinned broadly and said, "Sir!" Later they had prayers, the mistress reading loudly from the Bible. Then Edett and Gloria left, he carrying a kerosene lantern, she a plastic pail.

The screens were useless; I tucked my pants cuffs into my socks to keep the mosquitoes out while I typed at the dining table. Later, as I inserted a fresh sheet of paper, I heard footsteps and muttering near my front porch. Just as I became alarmed, a happy voice said, "Sir!" It was Edett and Gloria. She went into their house, but he left again.

The blades of the ceiling fan in the bedroom soared and dived, whizzed at breakneck speed, slowed to a crawl while the switch by the door sparked and buzzed. When I turned the fan off, the mosquitoes were merciless.

The neighbors arose at five. All of them. The little boys lined up to wet in the driveway, then staged an early-morning concert with their sticks and Nido cans. Edett and Gloria squatted behind the house. At seven, wearing a stiff nurse's uniform adorned with a plastic nameplate and several badges, her hair twisted up in short tight braids, the mistress of the house got into the Toyota, slammed the door, started and gunned the engine, honked the horn, and crashed the car across the loose boards over the ditch at the end of the drive.

Groggy from lack of sleep, I waded through mud and refuse at the market in search of flimsy aluminum pots, curtain material, a scrub brush, knives and forks, plates, a fan. The only fan I could find had a green light and a radio in its base. Fan, light, and radio operated simultaneously, or not at all.

The nurse returned at noon, honking as her wheels hit the boards and shouting "Edett! Edett!"

"Sister!" he answered.

And again at four: Smash! Honk! "Edett!"

"Sister!"

"You bought it? Bloody hell," Freddie said that evening after he had beaten me at squash for the first time.

"It was the only fan they had."

"Nonsense. What's happening to your game? You made stupid shots."

"No sleep. I'll be back on form Friday."

That night the green light glowed companionably, the radio muttered low static, the fan kept the mosquitoes off, and I slept.

I felt so good I took the next afternoon off to scrub the walls in the house. Soon, however, I realized the paint was coming off with the filth; I began to wash more gently, and just then Edett entered without knocking through the kitchen door.

"Good morning, Sir," he said. It was midafternoon. His teeth were flawless, his face rather flat. He was barefoot, about shoulder-high to me. His lappa was of the same material as their curtains. He wore a tattered undershirt and a wool stocking cap with Christmas trees printed on it.

"Good afternoon," I said.

"You will live here, I think."

"Yes."

"I am happy." His grin was enormous. He pointed at my scrub brush. "Sir. Is no job for white master." I laughed politely, not sure how to explain the egalitarian American work ethic.

Did we say more? I don't think so; he backed out of the house, still grinning. Yet at one o'clock the next day he was in my bedroom, making my bed; he threw my dirty clothes in the bathtub to soak, whistled happily, and asked for three naira to buy Milton and two naira for plantains and snails to cook for my dinner.

"I don't understand," I said. "Why are you doing this?"

"Morning make I work for Sister. Now you. Is good. Thank you. Thank you very much."

"How much do you expect me to pay you? I'm not a rich man, you know."

He laughed in delight. "Fifty naira fortnight. Is small-small for you, Sir. Thank you very much."

He scrubbed the walls, taking off the paint. He offered to wash the typewriter. A pot simmered in the kitchen, and that evening, sweating profusely from the pepper sauce, I ate rubbery snails and fried plantains.

"Hired him at a hundred naira a month, half time? You're an idiot," Freddie said Friday evening.

"I didn't hire him."

"Damned gullible Yanks. You make it hard on all of us."

"How much should I pay him?"

"For the work you'll get from him? Not a bloody kobo."

"He says he can't work on weekends because of what he calls 'job law.' I assume that's customary?"

Freddie shook his head wearily. "Idiot."

The nurse and Gloria woke me at dawn: a scuffling at my window, then a locust, I thought at first, but lower, more urgent, a humming punctuated by a *whish* and a thin, quick blow. The humming rose and intensified.

"Is that good thing? Tell me!" The nurse's voice crackled within inches of my ear. I sat bolt upright, certain she was beside the bed.

"Is that good thing or bad thing? Tell me!" I peeped through the curtains. Holding Gloria by the upper arm, the nurse struck her across the buttocks with a long green switch. The four boys filled the kitchen doorway, beaming. The girl twisted and writhed away from the switch, her mouth set in a tight stubborn line. But when the nurse—who was more muscular, I saw, than fat—shifted her attack to Gloria's legs the girl began to cry and beg in Efik, louder and louder. The nurse dragged her toward the kitchen door and slashed her ankles viciously, sending her hopping and bawling past the shouting boys. The nurse dropped the switch and went inside, still scolding. The boys fought over the switch.

I closed the curtain hoping it was a dream, so sudden and violent it had been. But Gloria's wailing, amplified by the concrete walls, continued with astonishing volume.

While I was making coffee at the kitchen counter, yet another girl, or woman, appeared. I opened the jalousies and there she was across the drive, leaning against the doorjamb, looking into their kitchen. Her dowdy, too-large, buttonless dress was open down her back to the cleft of her buttocks; her skin was muted satin. I poured Peak in my coffee, lightening it to the same shade. Arm akimbo, she rested with one leg bent, like a crane; in the kitchen the old woman muttered. The girl's eyes closed, her arm dropped straight; the dress edged off her shoulder, fell to her breast, caught, paused, slipped, paused, fell to her elbow, to her wrist and waist. In the house the little boys bickered. Sunlight coppered her skin. Without opening her eyes she hooked her thumb in the sleeve of the dress and tugged it up. It fell again, slowly. Something pulled at the hair on my leg. I glanced down: a gecko, no more than an inch long, was tangled there. I brushed it off. By the time she went inside, my coffee was cold. I had made it several shades too light.

I saw her again Sunday morning. Bending from the hips, she swept out the car tracks in the drive with a short grass-stem broom. At a shout from Edett—he worked weekends for the nurse, I noted—or some racket from the boys, she straightened and smiled, raised and retied her lappa, and called an answer or a reprimand in a low, unhurried voice. Her eyes were large, black, wide-set. Her lips opened generously over perfect teeth. Her breasts were pointed, like her face, like unripe bananas. She was beautiful.

I decided to call her the gazelle.

By midweek the pattern of my day was set. The nurse, whom I named Ratchet, awakened me almost every morning by beating Gloria. As I left for work I noted my pawpaws yellowing to ripeness. The boys shouted "Good morning, Sir" when I returned in the afternoon. They pounded the Nido cans incessantly. Ratchet returned at four: Smash! Honk! "Edett!" I had snails for dinner. Late each night Edett and Gloria left the house, returned.

On Friday (probably he was there to escape the children) Edett echoed the boys' greeting from high overhead in the almond tree. Pointing at my car, he said, "Sir, is not for good dirty."

I nodded. "Perhaps you can wash it—"

"Is no time. My brother come. Is very good for wash car."

Fifteen minutes later Edett and a gangling, drowsy man walked straight into my bedroom. "Sir," Edett said, "is my brother for wash car."

It is not easy to be authoritative in one's underwear. "I was going to play squash."

"Is all right." Edett scooped up my car keys from the dresser and gave them to his brother, who woke up, smiled blindingly, and vanished down the hallway.

"Wait! Where is he going?"

"No worry. Is license for drive."

"Why does he have to drive anywhere?"

"Here is not for good water wash car."

"I'm supposed to play squash."

"No worry."

At dinner I told Edett to cook something else besides snails, since their price had risen steadily from one to three naira. He had found excellent pawpaws, fifty kobo each. While he was washing the dishes, I opened the upper door of the fridge by mistake. The freezer was packed with ice cream bars.

Edett turned from the sink. "No worry, Sir; you no need ice part."

"But why is it full of ice cream bars?"

"Is no problem."

Freddie came by at eight, steaming. I apologized and lied about the car, saying it had broken down. After he cooled off, I showed him the ice cream bars.

"They're made with water straight from the public hydrants, or worse," he said. "Don't eat them, unless you fancy schistosomiasis."

"I won't."

"Is this Edett soaking your vegetables in Milton properly? This area has twenty-seven species of internal parasites, you know."

"I know." I lit a cigarette from my last one.

"When did you become a chain-smoker? You weren't smoking at all when you came here."

I said, "With twenty-seven internal parasites, why worry about smoking?"

Freddie glanced around the living room. "This place is filthy."

After Freddie went home, I saw Edett leave the other house alone. I had not seen him go out with Gloria. "Where's my car?" I shouted.

He raised his hands. "Is very slow, wash car." I decided to check on Edett's housekeeping: I left a cigarette butt behind the kitchen door.

The car was back the next morning, immaculate. His brother charged only two naira.

The gazelle's name, I learned, was Evangelina. From my kitchen window, with an intense mixture of pain and pleasure, I watched her leaning in their doorway or sweeping the drive. She seemed to do these things only on Saturday and Sunday.

I had called her the gazelle because of the sound of the word, its connotations of beauty, grace—I thought; but Saturday morning as I watched her it came to me, the association: a Renaissance painting, not a gazelle in it but a doe, an English deer with human, more than human eyes; what, where was that painting? That night I dreamed of presenting her at some hushed European court, her beauty a tawny, regal glow, I beside her, unassuming; her dependence on me clear to all.

The schoolgirl, the blocky, sullen one, never worked around the house. As I drove to work Monday morning—I had just noticed that my ripe pawpaws had been picked—I saw her and several other girls in school uniforms astride a sewer by the highway. They pulled aside the crotches of their underpants and fired away, like men.

Gloria I renamed the squashgirl Tuesday morning as Ratchet beat her, wielding the stick with a quick, strong wrist; a squash player's motion, skilled and vicious. The idea destroyed me on the court that afternoon. Freddie won so easily he was disgusted.

"What's happening to you?" he asked in the clubhouse afterward, pouring a shandy. "You're losing weight. Your cheeks are hollow."

I told him about the squashgirl and Ratchet, the beatings, but not that every swing of his racket had made me think of them.

"Pecking order," Freddie said. "In the scheme of the extended family, the girl is dead last at the moment. She's probably a poor relative of the nurse's from her village. She hasn't been circumcised like the other two girls yet. Not to worry, her turn will come."

"What about the boys? Doesn't she outrank them?"

"Certainly not; they're the nurse's. But she'll even the score on them, given a chance."

Freddie said Ratchet was one of the Deputy Minister of Culture's wives, his third. "Speaking of pecking orders, she's neither his first nor his latest; he has four, I believe. Not much status there."

Just after I came home, Edett's brother roared away in the Beetle, without asking. The next morning it was spotless, but the right rear fender was dented.

I called Edett from the other house. "Look at that!"

He bent, peered. "Sir. Is old."

"It is not old."

"No worry," he said. "Make I say my brother you pay one naira only."

In my anger I forgot my briefcase, and I scarcely noticed that Freddie had predicted correctly: the squashgirl whipped one of the boys after Ratchet went to work, and she was chasing another when the old woman came to his rescue.

Returning after lunch for my briefcase, I found Edett at my kitchen door lecturing three boys with cool-boxes balanced on their heads. He glanced at me, grinned, said "Sir!" to me and "Go now!" to the boys. As they reached the street, they began to shout, "Good ice cream! Good ice cream!"

"So you are selling the ice cream," I said.

"Sir, give me six naira for Milton."

"I thought it was three."

"Now is six." He began sweeping the kitchen.

As I tossed my briefcase in the Beetle the schoolgirl, sullen as usual, plodded by carrying an armful of books. Suddenly she straightened and smiled.

"Good afternoon, Sir."

"Good—" I stopped, not wanting to believe what at that instant was very clear: it was the gazelle. She—Evangelina—was the schoolgirl. Smile, voice, eyes—there was no doubt.

"You have a typewriter," she said.

"Yes."

"You are a secretary."

"No, I—actually, I'm an economist, a management consultant. I just type—"

"You are a secretary." She smiled again. "I am happy to see your typewriter. I learn it at school. Tomorrow I will come."

"Yes, certainly. You are welcome—at what time?"

"Four o'clock."

I watched her clump up the steps and into the house, stunned to think of the metamorphosis between the front door and kitchen door, where the gazelle would emerge barefoot in lappa or buttonless dress, graceful and lovely; even more stunned to think she would be in my house.

The next afternoon I watched the drive forever, and forever again. Edett washed my clothes in the bathtub and hung them in the drying area, whistling all the while. I looked in the freezing compartment of the fridge; it was full of ice cream bars. The cigarette butt was still behind the door. At last, at five, she appeared on their kitchen step; I opened my door before she could knock, and then she was at my table in my chair in her buttonless dress, pecking hesitantly at my ancient Royal while I hovered, fearful that the dream, the bubble would burst. The dress slipped and fell; she tugged it up unconsciously. She could not find the margin release; I put my hand on her shoulder as I showed her, and she did not flinch. Her skin was polished stone, dark, cool, and smooth even to my sweaty touch.

She said she would come again Friday.

She did not. It rained all day; in the morning, on orders from Ratchet, the squashgirl stood for an hour in the driveway in the downpour, crying loudly and steadily.

While waiting for the gazelle, even after I knew it was hopeless, I asked

Edett, "Where do you and Gloria go at night? After the others have gone to bed?"

"Go for snails." He turned away. "Bring clothes now."

"Just a minute. Did you sell those snails to me?"

"Is all right."

"You told me the price went up."

He raised his hands helplessly. "Sir, is market."

I slammed the door as I left, late for squash. I started the car, glanced up at a second tier of green fruit in the pawpaw tree, shifted to reverse, looked up again, leaped out, and ran back into the house.

"The pawpaws! Did you sell me my own pawpaws for fifty kobo each?"

"Is market, Sir."

"I suppose the six naira for Milton was due to the market too."

He nodded sadly. "Is market."

The next morning I was awakened by the boys' crying under my window; Edett was shaving each one's head with a bare double-edged blade while the child squirmed on an upturned Nido can placed on a chair. That afternoon Ratchet's husband arrived. He parked his Mercedes behind her Toyota. Tall, portly in a vested suit, he lined up the boys and the squashgirl for inspection before dinner, the boys naked, their heads freshly shaved, the squashgirl in her tattered, dozen-sizes-too-large dress. Ratchet slapped her sharply when she mumbled a reply to his question. I heard them— Ratchet and the Deputy Minister—late into the night, her ringing, coquettish laughter. Sunday morning she followed him to his car speaking in Efik, her voice wheedling, then whining. The old woman hobbled behind, wringing her hands. Ratchet's voice rose as he started the car. He laughed and drove away.

I was in love with the gazelle.

Her voice was like the taste of mango: a spreading richness. She typed at my typewriter, at my table. I was careful not to make her self-conscious, not to let her see my intoxication as her dress or lappa fell, as the slanting light through the jalousies lit and darkened her slender neck, the hollows of her shoulders. But Edett knew. Often I pulled my eyes from her to meet his, to see him smiling, knowing.

In my mind I draped ivory velvet against her coffee skin, or black silk. Massive circlets of gold burned over her sharp breasts.

I learned that Edett was married. Irritated that he had been watching us, I asked him one afternoon after the gazelle had left, "Where do you go each night?"

"Go my house, Sir."

"You do not sleep here?"

"Is not for my house." He grinned. "Go sleep wife. Is for better."

She was in my house every weekday for two weeks. I was as in a slow-frame film: each day, my hands on her bare shoulders, I read admiringly the paragraphs she had typed; once she leaned her head against my shoulder as I reset the margins; once she flinched and drew back, but only momentarily, when the hair of my arm touched her breast as I reached for the space bar.

I forgot both squash days with Freddie the second week. The following Monday he finally agreed to set an appointment for Friday: "The last bloody time if you miss."

The gazelle did not come Tuesday. While I paced the kitchen, I put a second cigarette butt behind the door.

On Wednesday she said, "I think you will give me this typewriter."

Her smile, voice pervaded me. Her hair was tied in seven short, stiff braids, as the women did there. I had never thought them beautiful before. "Perhaps I will," I said.

For two hours the next morning, first in her lappa, then in her uniform, Ratchet chased the squashgirl around the Toyota. She rested often on the kitchen step, panting and scolding. The boys found their own switches and struck the girl as she passed. The old woman tried to help, but the squashgirl easily eluded her. Finally the gazelle darted from the house and caught her. By then Ratchet was late for work and could give the bawling girl only a superficial beating.

When I came home at noon a young woman was kneeling by the front door, a tray containing two smoked goat haunches balanced on her head. I assumed Edett was buying meat from her and started to protest—Freddie had warned me about the goat-meat vendors, and indeed the haunches were matted with flies—but Edett said quickly, "I no buy, Sir." Then I saw that she was counting out stacks of ten-kobo pieces to him.

After she left I said, "She sells goat meat for you?"

"Is my wife, Sir."

While I was trying to nap—the boys were banging at their Nido cans—I heard Edett arguing loudly. Again he was at the front door, again with a woman balancing a tray of goat haunches.

"—Seven, eight!" He pointed at the stacks of coins, then snapped something in Efik. The woman, taller than he, heavy-boned, answered angrily and shook her finger at him without dislodging the tray.

"Make you—" Edett began, then, seeing me, smiled. "Go now!" he said to the woman.

She strode away, muttering. I said, "She also sells goat meat for you?"

"Is my wife, Sir."

"You have two wives?"

"Yes."

"I have heard that only rich men have more than one wife."

He laughed loudly, then pointed at the Beetle. "Tonight is for wash."

"Your brother just washed it yesterday."

"Is not for good dirty."

The second tier of pawpaws was nearly ripe.

I kept my date with Freddie on Friday. The gazelle did not appear, and after the usual pacing, noting that the freezer was packed with ice cream bars, and adding two more cigarette butts to the two already there, I forced myself to arrive at the club on time.

After we played—Freddie won—he asked a strange question: "What is the license number of your Beetle?"

"I don't know."

"Let's have a look."

I suspected I was about to learn something I didn't want to.

He stood before the car nodding, thumbs hooked in the waistband of his shorts. "Have you been lending your car out?"

"No. But Edett's brother takes it to wash it. Perhaps you saw—"

"What's your odometer reading?"

"About 15,000 kilometers." I leaned in the window, then staggered back. "It shows 26,000."

Freddie kicked the front bumper. One end sagged from the raffia strips holding it to the frame. "Your car is being used as a taxi."

I knelt and lifted the loose end of the bumper uncertainly.

Freddie said, "You ought to get out of this place."

My neighbors' house was dark when I came home. "Edett!" I shouted. No answer. I stood slump-shouldered. The bumper stuck out the window on the passenger side.

"Edett!"

Something rustled overhead. I peered up into the darkness. It was the squashgirl, her legs locked around the pawpaw trunk, the skirt of her huge dress heavy with pawpaws.

She said, "Is not for here, Sir."

"I can see that."

We stared at each other in the gloom before our dark houses, I bent with weariness, her face so gaunt her teeth protruded. Finally she snapped off the last of the plump, oblong fruit and slid down the trunk.

"Sir!" she called as I trudged into the house. "Make you buy pawpaw? Fifty-fifty kobo."

Edett had left a few shriveled carrots soaking in a pan of Milton on the kitchen counter. I glanced at them, then looked more closely: mosquito larvae swam, dove, and somersaulted in the pan. They looked very healthy. I grabbed the bottle—the cap was off—and emptied it into a bowl. It was densely populated with swimming things.

"Edett!" I screamed. I wondered if I would live through the night, wondered how many internal parasites were already devouring me.

There were eight cigarette butts behind the door.

I dreamed of the gazelle dressed in ivory velvet, her fingers cool as ivory on my arm as I presented her, regal and beautiful, in some hushed—but

Freddie kept breaking in and saying, "We are, after all, all of us squash-girls." I objected strongly. Freddie did not say such things, even in my dreams. I thought the gazelle might have said it, so, even as I tugged her arm and reminded her of our solemn moment, for her mind seemed to be wandering, and as I protested the interruption by Freddie, I myself inter-rupted to claim that the gazelle had spoken.

I called for Edett at daybreak, but he replied through the burglar bars of Ratchet's kitchen window, "Very busy, Sir." I made coffee, but my hands shook so much I kept spilling it. I went out in the drive and shouted, "Edett! Come here!"

At last he came out, grinning. The gazelle emerged behind him, retying the knot of her lappa. The squashgirl peeped over the heads of the boys in the doorway, and Ratchet and the old woman were at the dining room window.

"Sir—" he began.

"I am sacking you," I said. "I am sacking you as of this moment."

He grasped my hand and shook it. "Is all right, Sir. I am happy." He gestured at the gazelle. "Soon is my three wife Evangelina."

"Your three wife—"

"I think you will give us a small-small gift. Is custom."

The gazelle blushed. Three boys bearing cool-boxes passed us silently and stopped by my kitchen door. I closed my eyes and saw an endless procession of regal women in ivory velvet with trays of goat meat balanced on their heads.

"I will give you a gift," I said; "I will give my typewriter to your new wife."

"Thank you, Sir. Thank you very much." Edett shook my hand again happily; then his face filled with sorrow. "Sir. Please, make you pay me one hundred naira. Is sack law."

WITCH

"Where are you going? Turn here!"

"Sah," Benjamin began, but he knew I wasn't having any of it, wasn't about to let him drive two miles out of the way to our compound just because a woman was sitting at the corner. He stopped and backed up slowly.

She was sitting exactly as she had been every day for the past week, stiffly erect on the white three-legged stool between her little stack of cardboard boxes and the speargrass along the roadside. She was thin, her gray scarf tight about her head and knotted behind, her skirt wrapper the same color, neatly draped and hiding her feet, which I supposed were bare. Her sleeveless dress had a faded yellow floral pattern. It was too large for her and hung slackly from her shoulders, the folds gathered in her lap beneath her clasped hands. Her skin was dull, old without wrinkles, just deeper than copper in tone, and the late afternoon sun glinted on the dark ridges of the three curving, parallel tribal scars beneath each cheekbone. She might have been thirty or forty, fifty—who knows? The raffia basket with its snug cover was beside her. Neither the basket nor her clothing showed any sign of the red dust that swirled along Kwa Road.

Three women with large trays of pineapples and pawpaws balanced on their heads were crossing the highway to avoid her. Their heads swiveled as they walked, their eyes never leaving her, but her face was toward the sun, unmoving. As we turned down the rough dirt lane, Benjamin had to swerve around two boys watching her from about twenty yards away, the smaller with a finger in his mouth, crying.

I said, "What's she been up to, Benjamin? Putting the whammy on somebody?"

"Na bad witch. She don kill plenty baby." He looked straight ahead over the steering wheel of the Peugeot, gunning it before shifting.

"Slow down. So she's a witch. But how do you know—" I stopped, knowing he didn't want to talk about her. Through the rear window, I saw the larger boy tug at the other's shorts, pulling him away.

* * *

After I had showered and changed to shorts I joined Mary on the patio in the lengthening shade of the almond tree. She was wearing her yellow swimsuit, and a thick paperback and her reading glasses were beside her. When Essien brought whisky for me, I said, "Something to drink, for a change?" Essien paused, his tray held chest high.

"No." Essien still hesitated, and she said, "Will you tell him to go? Doesn't he understand English?"

I said, "Thank you, Essien," and as he disappeared into the house, "He understands you perfectly well. He was being polite."

"He's as bad as any of them. They're always watching me. I look up and there are children peeking around the corner of the house or women looking over the wall. They talk about me all the time."

"How do you know that? Been studying Efik?"

"And they laugh, and stare. Like those!" As she pointed, small brown buttocks disappeared behind a clump of sugar cane.

"Why shouldn't they stare? We're novelties here, you know."

"Essien's as bad as any of them. He stares too."

A milky-white, nearly transparent lizard scurried across the patio, raced up the smooth green trunk of the almond tree, and vanished into the first tier of waxy leaves. I said, "Been swimming?"

"Do I look wet?"

"No." At home Mary swam every day in the summer, but here she complained about the tepid sluggishness of the water, about giant insects alive and kicking in the pool despite its heavy chlorination. She was tanned, but the flesh of her thighs and face was slack. She had lost weight; her halter was loose and wrinkled. She had taken to sleeping later and later, and more than once I had come home from work to find her still in bed, not ill, not reading, just sleeping.

"So what did you do? Read at the pool? Sleep all day again?"

"I read. Right here."

"Find the ring?" The day before she had complained about losing a birthstone ring the children had given her.

"No." Her eyes seldom left some point over the rubber plantation, beyond the thatched roofs outside the wall, over the bamboo thickets and tall raffia palms farther out. She said, "I suppose you would have said if there were any letters."

"No mail."

"Why don't they write? Can't they ever write?"

Around the servants' quarters behind the houses the children were shouting and playing as the day's heat eased; the high banter of the women came over the hollow "thock! thock!" of yam being pounded.

"We've been there before." I rattled the ice in my glass with its blue Afri-Dredge label. Company glasses, like the house, the club pool and tennis court, the compound and its stout wall topped with broken glass.

I said, "By the way, the witch is still at the corner."

"The woman?"

"The witch. I'd swear she hasn't moved all week. Looks straight down the highway. Doesn't even blink when we go by. Doesn't see us."

Mary put her hands between her thighs as if she were cold. "I wonder what she does at night."

"Sleeps there, I suppose. Maybe in the grass off the road. Or in the dust. Maybe she just sits there."

"What if it rains? What would she do?"

"Dry season. Harmattan. No problem."

She looked at me for the first time. "No problem." The corners of her mouth were drawn down oddly, making faint crescent-shaped lines in each cheek. After a moment, she said, "I hate the dust. You can feel it when you breathe. You can feel it all around you."

"No dust on you."

"It covers everything in the house."

"There were two boys watching her. The younger one was crying and the other pulling him away. Probably been teasing him about the bad old witch and scared the hell out of him. He looked like he was petrified."

"Why don't they take care of her? I thought everybody was supposed to take care of everybody here. Extended family, or whatever they call it."

"She's a witch, that's why. Nobody will go near her. No place to go."

"I think someone ought to do something," Mary said.

"Who, for example? Us?"

She was looking toward the rubber plantation again. "Why not?"

"Like what? Take her to the Wilsons' tomorrow night? What if she hexed Adrian's genitals off? Or caused the Harris baby to be stillborn?"

"You really don't care, do you?"

"There's lots of misery here. Why start with her? The kids you were complaining about have navels the size of my thumb. That's supposed to be a protein deficiency. Why not do something about them? There was a naked woman downtown today. Cars had to go around her. Standing bent over—"

"I don't want to hear about it."

"So why pick this one?"

"You don't even care if the children don't write."

"Of course I care. I can't make them write. Can't hold a gun at their heads. Essien!"

"They might as well be dead." Mary waited, twisting her hands together, while the steward set a fresh glass down for me. She said, "I wish I could find the ring."

"Misplaced it. It'll turn up."

"I think he took it."

"Essien? Not a chance." Essien had been an Afri-Dredge steward fifteen years; he'd worked two years for me before Mary came over.

"Why do you always take his side?"

"Who's taking sides?" I said. "I'm just telling you what I know."

"Sometimes I get sick of what you know."

The sun was reddening, the disc sharply outlined behind the harmattan dust and the Atlantic mist, above the dark rubber trees. In the village beyond the wall drumming had started, and some of the children in the servants' quarters were marching now to their own impromptu music, an intricate pattern of sound coaxed from mackerel tins, sticks, a whitened tortoise shell. They pranced across the lawn of the next house, saw us, and swung away. And then like a curtain drawn it was dark.

* * *

When we came home from Harbourworks the next evening—again I had to force Benjamin to drive past the woman—I could see trouble a block away. Essien was waiting by the driveway, beside him a thin, gray-haired man, shirtless, barefooted, wearing a bright red lappa with a huge knot at the waist. On the far side of the drive was a semicircle of thirty or forty children, a few adults among them. Mary was on the porch.

"Now what?" I said as I got out.

Mary pointed at Essien. "He stole my ring! I *know* he took it!"

I turned to Essien. He said sternly, his eyes meeting mine, "Sah. I am no t'ief. I bring juju man." Benjamin, who had gotten slowly out of the car, quickly moved away from us.

I looked at the man, who seemed more interested in a paper bag he was holding than in us. I nodded. "All right. How much?"

"Ten-ten naira," Essien said. "Twenty naira."

I took a ten-naira note from my wallet and handed it to Essien. He put it with his own crumpled note and gave it to the man, who put the money in his bag.

"What are you doing?" Mary said. "I told you, this—"

"This is a juju man," I said. "It's the custom. You've accused Essien. He must clear himself, or he'll be out of a job. So he called in a juju man to find out what happened to the ring."

"Oh God," Mary said, watching the man in the lappa, who had taken a dingy pouch and some twigs and grass stems from the bag and was coming slowly toward the house, "I think I'm going crazy. Or you are. You act as if you believe in him."

"Essien believes in him," I said. "The fact that he called him is enough for me to know he didn't take it."

The man walked past Mary into the house, closing the door behind him.

"What's he—this *person*—in *our* house!" Mary protested, trembling; "You let him—"

"I told you," I said. "We just wait." And so we did. The crowd along the drive was silent, although it continued to grow. Essien had not moved; Benjamin stood by the open door of the Peugeot.

In about ten minutes the man came out. He walked past Mary and me, then whirled, pointed at Mary and said something in Efik, harshly. The children began to giggle.

"Benjamin," I said; "What does he say?"

"Sah," he stammered, "dis juju mahn 'e say 'e say ahm—"

"What?"

"'E say Madame don take ahm ring. Madame t'ief own ring."

Mary looked at Benjamin, at the juju man, at me as the giggling along the drive became laughter.

I said, "Mary—"

"You!" she screamed, then she folded like a dropped garment, and I caught her as she fell.

*   *   *

I found the ring immediately in the dresser under some of Mary's blouses, not hidden, I thought, just dropped there. Mary did not move from the bed for two hours, but when I suggested we skip dinner at the Wilsons', she shook her head, got up, and began to dress.

After she had dressed, I handed her the ring. She looked at it and began to tremble. "It's not fair."

"The main thing is you got the ring," I said.

She put it on. "That's not the main thing at all."

The woman was still there, yellow-gray in the splash of the headlights. Mary twisted in the seat to watch her as we turned onto Kwa Road. "I know," she said; "oh, I know very well."

I spent most of the evening huddled with Adrian Wilson and the other Harbourworks men, working out where we were to move the dredging operation next. Mary was quiet while the talk flowed around her—several times I looked up to find her eyes on me—and when we drove home she said nothing about the gray figure on the corner. Out over the harbor lightning flashed along the edge of a cloud mass, and she asked if it would rain.

"That's just heat lightning. No rain."

But after we went to bed it did rain, one of those incredible tropical bursts that come even in the dry season, that flood the streets and wash away the mud huts and hammer on the corrugated metal roofs.

Mary started crying.

"For Christ's sake." I switched on the bedside lamp.

She was sitting up, her hands twisting in her lap. "I can't stand to think of her out there."

"So she'll get wet. Or maybe she won't, if she's really a witch. This is the tropics. She won't freeze."

"There alone. It's not right." Her face again had that queer grimacing expression, pulling darkly etched lines around her mouth. She sat tensely, as if expecting a blow. Her nightgown had slipped off one shoulder.

"Where do you want her to be? They poured acid over a witch in a bush village last week. And staked another on an ant trail. Driver ants."

"Can't you see what I mean? Not the rain. She's *lonely*. I just wish I could talk to her."

"You can't talk to her. She doesn't know a word of English."

"I don't mean that. I mean *feel* with her. Help her feel—know I know she's alive, she's a person."

"Try to understand where you are. Stop trying to lay on your college psychology where you don't know what's happening."

"You're the one who doesn't understand. She came from somewhere, she must have had friends, a husband, children."

"What if she's really a witch? You think those boxes are full of lace doilies? Maybe she's got fresh monkey paws and human skulls in them. Maybe the basket's full of green mambas. Or potions to shrivel legs."

"Stop making a joke of it!" She sobbed, her body shaking; her hands writhed in her lap as if trying to burrow there, and the gown slipped down from her breast.

"All right." I pulled the gown up. "But you think she thinks the way you do. You don't know that. Witches are as real to people here as supermarkets are back home. You think that woman doesn't believe she's a witch? How do you know she's not there because she *wants* to be, for God's sake? How do you know she's not doing business there?"

"You don't even think she's human."

"I'm saying that where she is, in this place, she's a *witch,* goddammit! When are you going to learn where you are? Didn't the juju business teach you anything?"

I switched off the light and turned away from her, listened to the rain roaring on the roof for a couple of minutes, and dozed off. A clap of thunder woke me up about an hour later, and I knew—you know after so many years—that Mary wasn't in bed. I turned the light on again, looked around, puzzled, and then it hit me that the chair by the bed was gone.

"Oh, Christ," I groaned.

I put on my boots and got two of the slickers that we wore on the dredge from the closet. Then I started up the lane.

I hadn't lied to Mary: the rain was warm. It came straight down, deafening and blinding. In the flashes of sheet lightning I could see the road and the rivulets running at my feet, but I didn't see Mary and the woman until I stumbled between them.

The woman seemed—some trick of color, the lightning, I thought—not even wet. Mary was sitting on the bedroom chair facing her, hands in her lap, erect but somehow relaxed—I remember thinking in the confusion, *sedate*. The rain had flattened her hair about her head, and her gown was down to her waist, the straps loose below her elbows.

"Mary!" I took her arm and tried to pull her to her feet. "This is crazy! Come on!"

"Go on back," she said.

Behind me the woman shouted in a rasping voice that prickled my scalp, and I released Mary and turned to her. She bent toward me, her face yellow in the lightning's glare, raised her arm and pointed at me, and suddenly I felt the rain icy along my bones and heard my teeth rattling.

*   *   *

When I awoke I was sweating unbearably, still in the slicker and boots. The bed was soaking wet. I sat up and struggled with the slicker and with the gap in my memory between what I had seen and where I now was, groping for some detail—the rain stinging my face, the sound of my boots sloshing—as I stumbled back down the lane. Nothing.

Mary was sitting on the patio, fully dressed. The sun was just up, a dim, whitish circle resting on the dark line of the rubber plantation.

I said, "Do you want to go home? I'm willing to go if you want to."

"No," she said, putting a gray scarf over her dry, neatly combed hair and knotting it behind, "no, I don't mind staying."

Two small heads peeked out from the clump of sugar cane, but she seemed not to notice them, her eyes on the white sun low in the east. I backed slowly away from her and into the house.

THE RUNNING SCORE

"Eggs are fifteen kobo each," Weldon Dittmar said.

"Can you imagine?" Verna Dittmar asked. "A quarter apiece for eggs!" The Dittmars smiled, anticipating Lewis Herring's amazement.

"I'm very grateful for your hospitality," Lewis said, not for the first time; "I'll be happy to help out—"

"No, no." Weldon held up his hand. "NEPA reimburses us."

"Don't worry." Verna smiled again. "We're experts at coping."

It was the Dittmars' smiles, not the insane traffic or the venders thrusting smoked fish in his face, that made Lewis nervous his first day in Onitsha. Smiles that said, "Yes, we're suffering too, but we must do the Lord's will, so we are here, and happily here." When they smiled, even in the dimness of the small bulb over their dining table, Lewis felt he should see their faces illumined by a ray beamed down just for that moment.

He had been met at the airport by a young Englishman, Nick Sandlin, from the Nigerian Electric Power Authority who told him, "NEPA is short of housing, so newcomers must wait until a flat becomes available. In the meantime, Dr. and Mrs. Dittmar have graciously offered to take you as a guest in their home. They are also Americans. They teach at Calvary College here."

The Dittmars lived in a duplex. From the living-dining room a hallway led past two bedrooms, the smaller of which Lewis would use, a bathroom and separate shower, a drying area for clothes, a pantry with a padlock on the door, and a storage room. At the far end was the kitchen, from which a smiling Verna had made numerous trips as she brought food to the table. It was at least twenty-five yards away.

Lewis said the arrangement seemed inconvenient.

"It is," Weldon agreed. He tilted his head at a benevolent angle that said, "I will now enlighten you." Lewis, thinking it came from a lifetime of teaching, had already gotten used to it. "But in a tropical country you want the heat of the cooking stove as far away as possible. Also, most people here employ servants, and they don't care how far the servants have to walk. Many Americans, of course, feel uneasy having servants. Certainly Verna and I do."

"I can take care of my own kitchen, thank you very much." A few notes of Verna's high laugh preceded and followed her remark.

37

The Dittmars had been in Onitsha five years. They had survived two military coups.

"The secret is to stay home till it's all over," Verna said.

They had worked in Sierra Leone, Liberia, Mozambique, Zimbabwe when it was Rhodesia, and Sri Lanka when it was Ceylon. Except for home leaves, Verna had, in fact, spent all her adult life outside the United States. She had married Weldon when she was his student at a small church school in Missouri.

"He robbed the cradle," Verna said.

Weldon assumed a sly expression. "I neglected to tell her until after the wedding that I had taken a job at a mission school in Ceylon."

"So I completed my degree by hook—"

"But mostly crook," Weldon finished. He taught courses in religion and philosophy, Verna in home economics. An aunt had left a small farm in Missouri to Verna; they planned to retire there in a few years.

"We won't be able to make a living on it, so we have to save now," Weldon said.

They laughed a good deal. Lewis knew he was watching a well-rehearsed act, but it was nevertheless interesting. Although they kept the stage, they found out that he had grown up in Nebraska and worked at electrical installations on the East Coast in the Norfolk area and in the Northwest in Spokane and Seattle, and that he had three grown children by a marriage which had ended in divorce many years ago.

"Even if we had wanted a divorce, we'd have been too busy." Verna's trill sounded again.

"We have no children, and thousands," Weldon said.

Verna's arm swept over the table. "Our Christmas cards covered three walls this year."

They had sat down to dinner at six-thirty. Cries from the street caught Lewis's attention several times, and he turned to watch the venders through the jalousies of the window overlooking the porch. Many were children with trays of pawpaws or loaves of bread balanced on their heads. Around seven the cries abruptly stopped; Lewis looked again and saw that the equatorial night had fallen.

When Verna rose to clear the table, Lewis took his plate and silverware to the kitchen before she could stop him. He offered to help with the washing and drying, but Verna shooed him out.

"This is my territory," she proclaimed.

Weldon said to Lewis, "She'll be finished in no time, and then the real business of the evening will start."

The real business was Scrabble. Weldon brought a battered maroon Scrabble box and a three-ring binder with heavy covers from their bedroom. He took a Scrabble dictionary and a standard dictionary from a bookcase in the living room and arranged the books, the Scrabble board, a canvas bag of tiles, letter racks, and an egg timer on the coffee table.

The distant clatter of dishes stopped, Lewis heard the toilet down the hallway, and then Verna joined them. Weldon, who was sitting on the couch, had been studying the notebook while they waited. It had stout rings of the type Lewis remembered on electric company records in pre-computer days. Verna sat in a chair, folded her hands, and looked at Weldon expectantly.

He held up the notebook. "What I have here, Lewis, is the record of our lives."

"Oh, not our lives," Verna protested.

Weldon tilted his head. "We've always worked where there was no television, often no radio. Sometimes we were the only English-speaking people for miles around. So on our first overseas assignment, which was in Ceylon over thirty years ago, we began playing Scrabble. We play at least one game every evening, sometimes two."

Verna put in, "And on weekends during the rainy season, we've played as many as six in one day."

"As many as six. But what is really unusual—" Weldon thrust out the notebook, and Lewis saw two neat pairs of columns on each page, with occasional notations on the left side of the columns and, at intervals, a larger number on the right side—"what is really unusual is that we not only score each game, we also keep a cumulative score. And we have kept it for over thirty years."

Verna laughed exultantly. Lewis murmured, "That's incredible."

"Isn't it?" Weldon turned the pages. "It's all here, by year, month, and day. Would you like to know who won on April 16, 1961? Verna did. She used all her letters twice, in successive plays. She spelled *blackens,* and on the very next play *clicking*."

"And it hasn't happened since," Verna said.

"What's the score now?" Lewis asked. "Who's ahead?"

"Oh, he's been ahead of me for years." Verna rolled her eyes. "After all, he's a Ph.D."

"But not by much." Weldon turned the pages until the neat columns ended. "As of last night, Verna's score was 1,721,638 points. I have 1,722,512. With over three million points scored, we are less than a thousand apart."

"That is truly amazing," Lewis said.

Verna shook the canvas bag. "That's enough history! Lewis, I hope you're a Scrabble player. Won't you join us?"

"Wouldn't that break up your continuity? I don't want—"

"We've often had guest players." Weldon turned the pages. "Here. In 1965 Sister Madelyn played every night for two months."

"She was very good," Verna said.

Weldon thumbed pages again. "In 1972 Milton Speck played with us in Rhodesia."

"He couldn't spell *at all!*" Verna laughed shrilly.

Lewis said, "Let me watch you professionals for a few nights, and if I think I won't embarrass myself too much, I'll join in then."

The game was a relief. The Dittmars stopped smiling, bent forward, and focused on it with a concentration that made Lewis think of chess masters. Their eyes moved back and forth from the board to their tiles, flicking occasionally toward the little sandglass, the three-minute egg timer, which they observed strictly and skillfully. Their words seemed commonplace to Lewis: Verna started with *thorn,* Weldon followed with *clean,* connecting to the *n* of *thorn,* and then Verna put down *loaf,* making *to, ha,* and *of* with the *t, h,* and *o* of *thorn.*

"*Loaf,* Anglo-Saxon *hlaf,* is also the source of *lady,*" Weldon told Lewis. "The word *hlafdige,* 'loaf-kneader,' became *levedi* in early Middle English and later shortened to *lady.*"

They were a handsome couple, Lewis thought. Verna's angular face bespoke hardship, yet was still pretty; she was about fifty, not slender but trim in her frumpish housedress, her dark hair hardly touched by gray. Weldon, whom Lewis judged to be sixty, had a bit of a paunch; he was clean-shaven, his hair combed in elegant gray waves, his nose straight, his chin crisp and square.

They played silently, except for an occasional complaint about too many vowels or too few, and compliments when one or the other made a high score. Weldon wrote in the heavy binder on his lap with a fountain pen, announcing the score after every third round. Verna challenged when he played *mome* and lost her turn.

"*Mome,*" Weldon intoned, reading the dictionary: "Blockhead, fool."

Verna said ruefully, "That's what I am for challenging you."

At the end of the game, Verna finished her rack first and caught Weldon with several high-count letters, but she still lost by six points.

"If only I hadn't challenged," she moaned.

"You'd have won easily," Weldon agreed. He conducted a post-mortem, pointing out the triple-word and triple-letter squares they had missed. "If many of these are open and you haven't played the high-count letters like the *z* and *q* on triples, you haven't played very efficiently."

"He sounds more like an economist than a philosopher, doesn't he?" Verna said.

*   *   *

At work on Monday, Nick Sandlin said, "So. Are we compatible with the Christians?"

"They seem to be very pleasant," Lewis answered.

"It'll be lively there the next two years."

"Years?"

"NEPA never gives flats to us bachelors," Nick said. "I couldn't break that news your first day, could I? Have they told you how much NEPA is paying them to keep you?"

"No."

"Twenty naira a day; one of the perks you can get in a corrupt country."

Lewis said after a moment, "It doesn't seem like so much to me. They were telling me how expensive food is."

"They would. Most people here divide the money with the guest, but they won't. Make them furnish your beer and cigarettes and put some beef on the table instead of that stringy chicken."

But Lewis said nothing. The Dittmars seemed to him a good buffer to the culture he had stepped into from a Boeing 727. From the streets where Ibo mixed with pidgin English, where people wore everything from three-piece suits to lappas to nothing, where his own white face was most alien of all, he could retreat every night into a life that reminded him of his boyhood in Nebraska.

After dinner that evening Nick picked up Lewis and took him to the Niger Club, a long, low building with a rusty metal roof on a bluff above the river. A separate building housed a squash court, and there was a tennis court in the palm trees.

"You'll meet a good lot of Nigerians here as well as most of the ex-patriates, except for the likes of the Dittmars," Nick told Lewis. Over their second drink at the bar, Lewis filled out a membership form.

He got home just as the Dittmars were pouring their Scrabble tiles back into the canvas bag.

"Weldon won again," Verna said. "I had terrible letters."

Weldon said, "Once you reach a certain level of skill, there's a good deal of luck in Scrabble. You can't win with just o's and i's."

Lewis felt he should not set a pattern of leaving the Dittmars' table as if he were a customer at a diner, so he declined Nick's invitation to the club the next evening and stayed to watch the Scrabble game. Verna won handily, playing all her letters with *onrushing* for a fifty-point bonus and combining short words, Lewis thought, very cleverly.

Sitting at his host's left on the couch, he studied Weldon's letters. Twice he thought of the same word that Weldon played. When Weldon played *nerve,* Lewis had rejected that in favor of *verve,* which would have made more points.

Weldon would not allow Verna to play *quo.* She told Lewis, "I get *qua* and *quo* mixed up."

"*Qua* yes, *quo* no." Weldon closed the dictionary.

After they had played for an hour, Weldon brought a bottle of brandy and two liqueur glasses from the sideboard and invited Lewis to join him.

"Am I taking your glass?" Lewis asked Verna.

She flushed and shook her head. "That's Weldon's only vice." She turned a tile slowly in her fingers, stroking each corner as she studied the other letters on the rack. She forced an edge of the tile between the others, sliding them apart silently, then held another the same way. When nearly all the sand had fallen in the glass, she caught her lower lip under her teeth and put her word on the board. After replacing the tiles she had played, she held the canvas bag in the palms of her hands until Weldon took it.

Weldon had an evening class on Wednesdays. Lewis thought it would be diplomatic to be out of the house then, so he went to the Niger Club with Nick. He watched the Dittmars play on Thursday night.

On Friday evening he said, "All right. I'm ready to be the sacrifice, if you still want me to play."

"Good!" the Dittmars said in unison.

It wasn't just having a good mix of vowels and consonants, and of being able to form words from the jumbled letters, he realized; you had to fit them into the pattern, to play the high-count letters on the bonus squares, to use the double-word spaces not once but twice. You needed to know little words like *edh,* which Verna played and he had never heard of, and *adz,* little trick words like *la, ti,* and *ta.* The sand seemed to roar through the egg timer, and he lost one turn by not playing quickly enough. When he played *Zen,* Weldon disallowed it as a proper noun. He was drubbed.

"I thought I wouldn't be embarrassed, but I am," he said as Weldon totaled the scores. He had been placed to Weldon's right on the couch.

The Dittmars laughed. "You played well for the first time," Weldon said. "It's a good idea to study the Scrabble dictionary to learn the small words that'll get you out of tight spots."

"I'll do that."

                    *   *   *

Occasionally Lewis went to the Niger Club on nights other than Wednesdays, usually with Nick, although NEPA had furnished him with a Land Cruiser. He spent Saturday and Sunday afternoons at the club playing squash or billiards, or, sitting on the veranda, talking with expatriates from Ireland, Egypt, Venezuela, Poland—almost anywhere.

He went with Nick once, once only, to the Iroko Club, where loudspeakers boomed reggae, the beer was warm and overpriced, and prostitutes tugged at his arms.

He had soon experienced the extent of Verna's menu: stewed chicken, tuna casseroles, egg-drop soup, banana bread, canned ham and corned beef, plenty of fresh fruit. Her only African dish was fried plantain.

"Doesn't she ever try the fish or goat?" Nick asked. "The fish is excellent here, and goat meat makes the best curry."

"I don't think they like going into the markets."

"I'll wager you haven't tasted pepper soup or snails either. The snails here are big as your head."

Lewis didn't reply. He didn't want to tell Nick that he looked forward to the plain food, that it was a sort of refuge. One evening as Verna served him from a casserole, the memory of a heavy comforter from his childhood and of a particularly bitter Nebraska winter had come to him so strongly he had shivered.

Nick also criticized the Dittmars because they did not keep a servant. "It's a labor-intensive economy. If you make a good salary, you have a social obligation to hire others."

"They have a girl who washes clothes one morning a week."

"One bloody morning. Do they pay her in blessings or naira?"

*   *   *

During the hour before dinner while Weldon napped and Verna walked back and forth from the kitchen—she steadfastly refused his help—Lewis studied the Scrabble dictionary, aware of her quiet amusement. For several weeks the effort seemed wasted. There were never letters for the words he remembered, never words for the openings on the board. Gradually, however, he understood more about how English words were put together. He learned to spot workable combinations of consonants quickly, to look for suffixes like -ion and -ing. Quickly taking new tiles out of the canvas bag warm from Verna's hands, he learned to study the board while she and Weldon were playing, to anticipate and rank his options so that when his turn came the sand dropping in the glass wouldn't panic him. It did not chafe him that Weldon decided on the propriety of all the words; that was a given, the terms under which he came to the household, the game. Sometimes, however, he felt Weldon was too arbitrary, even harsh, in judging Verna's word choices.

He began to win occasionally, to his surprise and the praise and encouragement of the Dittmars. At the end of such games Weldon would hold out the notebook with his scores, a third column of figures added along one side, to show him by how much, with what play he had taken the lead for good.

As he improved he relaxed, discovering that he could sift out the possibilities of his letters without constantly bending over them and knitting his brows, that he could enjoy the game. He observed Weldon and Verna's play with new understanding. He began to realize that Verna was a relentless scrapper. She landed her high-count letters on the bonus spaces nearly every time, and when she drew low-count letters, vowels, *t*'s, *l*'s, and the like, she ran them parallel to another word or between words and made *lo, la, lot, pi, pa, pat,* chipping away and scoring more than Weldon with his *larrup* or *parley* or *decant*. She converted unlikely corners, apparent dead ends like *elm* and *leg* to *whelming* and *phlegm*. She usually went out first, sweeping the extra vowels from her rack with words like *aerie, union,* or *oilier*. She seldom left a fat opportunity for Lewis. Her specialty, he thought, was exploiting the triple spaces, making them work two directions, *of* one way and *if* the other. One night she made fifty points with *ex* and *xi*.

Weldon tilted his head. "*Ex* illustrates our English preference for short words; the meaning of *ex-wife* shifts to the prefix, and we drop the base word."

As he became a good player, as he observed, Lewis became aware that the real competition was between him and Verna. Weldon might win a round, and the next one too, or, with lucky draws, even a game, but he couldn't keep it up; he lacked Verna's resourcefulness, her relentless attack. One night when Weldon put down *azo,* Lewis saw on the other side of the board a triple letter box for the *z,* the connecting *e* of *power,* a spot for an *a,* the connecting *l* of *lava;* Weldon could have tripled his score with *zeal.* Lewis glanced up and was startled to find Verna's eyes meeting his for a moment. She too, he realized, had seen Weldon's mistake. His sudden rush of pleasure at this knowledge startled him again.

He studied Verna's technique and imitated it, saw ways to steer the game defensively, as she did, so that when he turned the board to Weldon there was never an easy bonus, the best play was a row or column out of reach. He began to win as often as either of the Dittmars.

One rainy Saturday afternoon when he skipped the Niger Club, they played three games. Between the first, which Lewis won, and the second, Weldon traded places with Lewis on the couch, moving him back to where he had sat when he first watched the Dittmars playing.

"So we don't ossify," Weldon explained.

Lewis won the second game too, and the third. From then on, though the scores were close, he won as many games as Verna and Weldon together.

Verna's shrill laugh was silenced when they played. Although a day's work was behind her and she was resting, her movements quickened. She spoke as much to herself as to Weldon and Lewis in a low, musing tone, unlike what Lewis thought of as the public voice she used at dinner. That she seldom smiled during the game seemed to him proof of her happiness then. Their eyes met often, hers and Lewis's, as Weldon played *colds* when *scold* would have doubled his score, *resign* when *reigns* would have tripled it. Lewis sensed no derision or malice in these looks, and at first no complicity beyond the acknowledgement that he or she would have done better. Sometimes, now that he and Weldon had exchanged places on the couch, he left an easy opening for Verna, one he could have cut off. He saw that she understood this too, what he had done for her, and was puzzled by it. Now he held the canvas bag cupped in his hands before passing it, wanting her to feel his warmth.

When the Niger Club announced a curry luncheon for a Sunday afternoon, Lewis invited the Dittmars to come as his guests.

"They say the club stewards are very good. It might be a nice change of pace," he said, meaning for Verna. So far as he knew, she had cooked three meals a day without missing since he had been there; he ate at the plant, but he knew the Dittmars came home for lunch.

He thought a shadow of wistfulness passed over Verna's face as she looked across the dining table at her husband. But Weldon, after considering a moment, tilted his head and said, "You know, we wouldn't fit in very well out there. But thanks for thinking of us."

Weldon bent over his plate again. Irked at his refusal, Lewis tried to meet Verna's eyes, but she laughed and told about her failure to describe macaroni and cheese to one of her classes.

At the club, Nick said, "Why invite them anyway? Speaking of wet blankets."

"I thought she would enjoy getting out of that kitchen."

"We're not falling for Mrs. Dittmar, are we? She's weathered well, given she's a century out of date."

"No, we're not," Lewis lied.

*   *   *

As he lay in the adjoining bedroom, Lewis strained to hear their sounds through the concrete wall, heard nothing. Sometimes he thought of going again to the Iroko Club with Nick, then chucked the idea in distaste. Now, when he left an easy play for Verna, she caught her lip under her teeth and thanked him with her eyes as if he had done some small courtesy for her, or, he thought, as if he had said, "You are beautiful tonight." They ran their words along each other's on the board, *leper* under *rube* to spell *re, up,* and *be; opt* over *dread* to make *or, pe,* and *ta.* When Verna took the bag from Lewis now, she held her palm against its warmth before she opened it.

None of this was enough. He wanted to hear that low tone in her voice, that intimate tone, wanted to hear it elsewhere besides over a Scrabble board.

And something made no sense. As his desire grew, so grew his puzzlement over the scores of the games. Gradually it changed to a suspicion that, at first, he pushed out of his mind; he didn't like it, wanted it to be baseless. It was too simple, right under his nose, to be credible. And too complicated. Nevertheless, as the days passed his suspicion hardened until it would not be denied.

Finally, during a game on a Monday night, he noted Verna and Weldon's scores carefully, listened as Weldon read them, and learned the truth. He checked again on Tuesday night as Weldon announced the scores after the third round, and then he checked no more.

"*Jaunty, gentle,* and *genteel* all originate from a single French word," Weldon said.

As Lewis watched Weldon in perplexity and anger, Verna's shrill laugh, her public laugh, broke through his bemusement, and her eyes, dark and apprehensive, caught his. He refused to acknowledge her warning at first; he intended to say something. But while Weldon read the scores a second time and then explained the paucity of English words beginning with *j,* Verna's warning became a plea, and Lewis said nothing.

*   *   *

On Wednesday night Lewis stayed after Weldon left for his class. Verna protested when he announced he would dry the dishes, but gave in good-naturedly. She spoke of her classes, he talked of the theft of huge crates of insulators from a NEPA site. Her high laugh accompanied his story and his attempts to stack the dishes in the right places.

"Thank you very much," she said as they finished. "That's the first time I haven't dried the dishes after a meal since we were on the plane coming back from home leave."

"It was my pleasure," he said. He turned her to face him, his hands lightly at her shoulders, and kissed her. He felt her neither respond nor recoil, saw neither desire nor shock, only mild surprise on her face.

She took his hands from her shoulders and turned toward the hallway. "It's still early. Why don't you go to your club? I have tests to grade."

And because there was no desire, no fear, no reaction at all, only—it seemed to Lewis—serenity, as if she had just done the dishes in the bland clatter of pans that ended any day, he was angered. He had not reached that intimate voice; she had passed through his action and him as she might through the hallway.

And because he could think of nothing else to say, he said, despising the smallness of it, "He cheats. You know that, don't you? If you get ahead of him he juggles the score. He doesn't change mine or his, but he takes away from yours."

She folded her hands uncertainly over her apron. After a silence, she said in the voice he had wanted to hear, "Wait in the living room."

He sat on the couch. She came from their bedroom carrying the notebook and a calculator and put them on the coffee table before him.

"Pick any page," she said, sitting in her usual chair; "any year."

He checked the scores on the column for March 12, 1958, tapping at the calculator keys; another column for a day in October 1970, another for a day in September 1982. Three added to seven made nine in her column, four to three six, forty plus forty seventy.

Lewis closed the book. "He's been doing it for thirty years."

"Yes."

"Have you always known?"

"Why do you think he changed places with you on the couch? You made it even harder for him to play than I did."

He looked at her wordlessly, remembering his and Weldon's thimble-sized glasses of brandy side by side on the coffee table, remembering Weldon's little word lectures, thinking of the three of them, their evenings of placid deception. His anger resurfaced, anger at her . . . *serenity,* he thought again, the word mocking him: that glass-smooth wall he had breached, and found a thicker one behind it.

In a rasping voice, he asked, "What do you think about it?"

"I don't think about it."

"I don't believe you," he said.

She shrugged. "What are they? Numbers on a page."

"They're more important to you than that."

She did not answer.

"Does he know that you know?" Lewis asked.

"In his own way," she said.

"Meaning what?"

"That he doesn't think about it either."

Lewis pointed at the notebook. "He called that the story of your life. It's the story of his cheating you every night."

"He just . . . keeps a difference there that he needs."

They were still seated, facing each other across the low table. Lewis said, "Tell me why you go along with it."

Frowning, she retrieved the notebook and calculator and then stood up, holding them in her folded arms. She said slowly, "I suppose because it's always seemed like the only thing to do."

Lewis watched her go into the bedroom, his anger changing to sadness. The glass-smooth wall changed too, seemed to him not so much a wall as time: years, decades, even centuries.

When she returned he said, "I'll go to the club."

"Yes. That's a good idea."

*   *   *

Lewis was on his second double whisky when Nick came from the billiards room to join him at the bar.

Nick said, "Bit late from vespers tonight, aren't we?"

"No comment," Lewis answered, and then the whole story tumbled out.

When he finished Nick called for another round and said, "There you are, old chap, one of your Puritans: a blinking blind-faithful wife."

"She's not!" Lewis blurted. "She's—" He stopped, baffled.

"Not what? Blind? Or faithful?"

"Not faithful," Lewis muttered. "But she is."

"Riddles." Nick studied Lewis. "She does for him at the scene of the crime, what?"

Lewis remembered the way she turned a tile, saw her catch her lip as he added a *t* to her *high,* as she played *took* under the *igh* of *thigh.* "Yes," he said, "when I'm there."

Nick chuckled so hard he spilled his drink. "Then play the bloody Scrabble game with her," he said. "She's giving you the best hour of her life."

*   *   *

Lewis returned to the house around eleven. Weldon was in the shower. Verna met him in the living room and asked, "Are you going to move out?"

"I think it would be best," he said.

"Yes, I suppose so." She blushed. Lewis felt his face redden too, and he looked regretfully at the coffee table. He would miss that, he thought, their words reaching to each other and joining on squares as soft as pillows. He would miss their game among the other games.

THINGS WE LOSE

I

When I retold the story of Danny and Marty Ransom's disastrous arrival at Harbourworks, I always explained that I had been a witness because Bob Mullin, the Olympic diver, had suffered complications with his Sunday morning hangover, namely, as Dr. Kumar diagnosed it, a concussion. Actually, I told two versions of what I saw at Mbopo Pier, but Danny and Bob heard only the first. Marty got the second one out of me, and she changed it so much I decided it was hers, not mine.

Bob had too much Champion beer and Irish whisky—and so did I—at the Barnsdalls' party. Around five in the morning he decided to sober up in the pool. He made a clean dive, fully clothed, into two feet of water. I fished him out, his head all bloody, and at eight o'clock he was still in Kumar's clinic. That was when Monday Obuku, Bob's assistant on the crane at Mbopo Pier, got me out of bed. A freighter had docked, and he couldn't get the crane engine started.

My driver, Paul, had the keys to the Land Cruiser, but he wasn't to be found, meaning that he had probably sneaked off to his "place," his village. I couldn't think of anyone I cared to wake up at that hour—the whole compound had been to the party—so Monday and I went by the warehouse to get my toolbox, and then we passed the security guards at the back gate of the compound and walked to the pier. It was a gray, hazy morning like most others in the dry season, already hot, and the women by their huts along the road and spreading up the hill above the river had tugged their lappas up over their breasts. People who work in the heat know you keep cool with more clothing, not less.

It wasn't pleasant walking. With a hangover in the tropics, you wake up itching from your own sweat and dehydrated, and the air is a soggy hand over your face. Monday wasn't enjoying himself either. He had already been given hell by the crew waiting to unload the freighter, and I knew he was worried about running the crane without Bob there. He was about thirty, good-looking, medium height, slender face with a skimpy beard curling tightly under his jaw, light brown skin. He had two wives, one at his quarters on the hill overlooking Mbopo Pier and another, his first, back in his "place."

The good thing about a hangover in the tropics is it doesn't last long. By the time we had walked the half-mile to the pier, I had sweated out the worst—my toolbox was heavy—and was feeling better. Just sleepy.

We threaded our way through the crowd, two or three hundred venders, touts, taxi drivers, messengers, day-laborers, amputees, a few drunks, employed and unemployed in lappas or rolled-up trousers and tattered shirts, all lounging along the riverbank in the shade of a few palm trees, a mammy wagon, and a retaining wall. All were male except for a few women selling oranges from trays balanced on their heads and two or three tall, beautiful beggar women from Chad. All of them said *"mbakara"* perfunctorily as we passed. I had been around too long to arouse any interest, even among the beggar women.

Mbakara is one of those words with a hundred shades of meaning, depending on who's using it and what mood he's in. It once meant—so my boss, Harry McIvor, claimed—"white master"; but not in Nigeria in 1982, twenty years after independence; now it meant anything from amazement in some bush village where no one had ever seen a white man, to a simple statement of fact, "you're white," to "white asshole." And worse.

The freighter had a Dutch flag. There were the usual crates to be unloaded, crates of the things Third World countries pay outrageous prices for, engines, cable, insulators, sausage, Guinness stout, Tabasco. There was also a Toyota van on the deck. It was packed above the windows with what looked like household goods—I could see a television and pots and pans, even potted plants—and under a plastic sheet on top were a pair of bicycles, a charcoal grill, and maybe toolboxes. I remembered then that Harry had said the other electrician he had hired was coming down the coast by freighter from Sierra Leone, where he'd been working. That—traveling by freighter—had struck us as odd, and even odder the fact that the man had said he had tried to drive to Nigeria from Sierra Leone but couldn't get a visa for one of the little countries on the route—Togo maybe, or Dahomey. Most of us flew, period; you worked in Harbourworks, and when you set foot elsewhere, it was in England or Germany, Ohio or Texas. Nothing in between.

As usual, starting the engine on the crane was a matter of tinkering with the fuel line. It should have taken me about five minutes, but I kept dropping wrenches and sweat dripped on my glasses, so I needed thirty, plus swearing. I hated working on the crane; the big diesels on the dredge, where I spent most of my time, were in the shade. Here, the sun was just a gray ball behind the haze, but it made whatever metal it struck too hot to touch, and it was searing my back.

"*Mbakara*," Monday said.

I looked up, knowing he wouldn't call *me* that.

"Da." He pointed toward the pier.

I heard a murmur running through the crowd, louder and livelier than when Monday and I had passed. It was a couple, the man thin and maybe six feet tall, the woman half a head shorter. He wore a loose shirt in a brown tie-dye pattern that seemed to be sold all over the country, and she had on a loose-fitting dress, probably African too. I couldn't see their faces. They made their way through the crowd, the center of a tight little circle that moved with them. The circle consisted of the touts, each trying to steer them toward his man's taxi. The beggar women also sent their children to tug at the woman's dress and the man's shirt or, if he had any, the hair on his arms. It's an experience, passing through that sort of mob at an airport or pier, that has turned many foreigners around and sent them home. The touts are experts at unnerving their victims; they press against you, pull at your arms, grab your bags, whisper or shout in your ear, and push their faces right up in yours, eight or ten of them. Meanwhile you're aware of the "*mbakara-mbakara*" murmur surging ahead of you like a wave; it stops with you, turns with you; you can't escape it. But the touts are the worst. I've seen American women go into hysterics at Lagos Airport, just stop, close their eyes, clench their fists, and scream at the top of their lungs while the touts laugh; I've seen men in business suits suddenly start whirling like some wild dancer, trying to brain someone with their bags. And the touts laugh.

But this couple moved ahead steadily. They didn't huddle against each other as foreigners often do, didn't shout or wave their arms. They knew what they were doing, I saw, and so did the touts, who began falling away as the couple walked out on the pier toward the unloading area, where there were Harbourworks security guards. The children of the beggar women gave up too, and finally the man and woman stood alone, waiting for their van.

"Now," I said to Monday. He tried again, and the engine started. The crew on the freighter began yelling at Monday, so I gathered my tools and climbed down out of his way. I walked behind the crowd until I found a shady spot in the open door of one of the storage sheds, and then I stopped to watch, thinking that if Harry McIvor didn't show up soon, the couple would need my help to get past the Harbourworks security guards and find their housing.

After Harry told us about this electrician and his attempt to drive from Sierra Leone, I looked at a map. It wasn't far, not as far as across Texas, probably, but distance wasn't the point. At Harbourworks we regarded the few miles' drive into Georgetown as dangerous, and all of us tried to get out of driving to Port Harcourt, seventy miles away, where we had another dredging operation. The road was terrible, for one thing; the potholes could take an axle from under a Land Cruiser, and the pavement had disintegrated in some stretches. During the rainy season chunks of the highway just sank; one of the chiefs from Georgetown had driven into a hole like that in his Mercedes, and a truck landed on top of him. Bush taxis—Peugeot station wagons or Toyota vans crammed with passengers—careened down the middle of the road, giving way only to the big trucks, the mammy wagons. On every trip you saw freshly wrecked and burned-out cars, sometimes not even pushed off the road. And there were road-blocks manned by local police or state police or soldiers, you were never sure, just as you were never sure if their rifles or machine guns were loaded.

And here was this electrician and his wife who wanted to drive through Liberia, the Ivory Coast, Ghana, Togo . . . the names of the cities on the map—Abidjan, Accra, Lome—were familiar to me because I had been on planes that had landed at their airports, yet I knew nothing about them. I wanted to talk to this couple, to find out if this was a sudden notion they'd had or if they knew what they were doing, had done things like this before. Even coming down the coast on the freighter was unheard of to people in Harbourworks. It stirred something in me; I thought of *The African Queen* and Dinesen's East African stories, of descriptions I'd read, history and fiction, of ships lying off the Gold Coast, Ivory Coast, Slave Coast, of half the sailors dying of malaria without even going ashore. . . . Chloroquinine had eliminated some of that danger, but standing on the deck of a freighter seemed both free and dangerous to me, infinitely more so than being strapped in a Pan Am seat, given a blanket and a drink, and fed every four hours.

Monday unloaded several crates, and then the freighter crew fastened a sling around the Toyota van. It was much heavier than the crates. When the cable tightened, the crane engine coughed and died before the sling had moved the van. The crew on the boat shouted and waved their arms. I groaned and bent for my toolbox, but the engine restarted immediately. Monday gunned it, and the sling jerked upward. As he swung the van toward the dock it tilted rearward and began to slip out. The crew, and I, shouted uselessly. Monday swung it back toward the ship. The van hit the bow above the far rear tire. A jagged line raced around the corner of the body at the rear, angling upward toward the windows. The shrill sound of metal grinding and tearing against metal came to us, and then the van slid out of the sling and dropped into the water. For an instant, an instant only, it bobbed upright in the water, as if it would float. Just as I realized that the jagged line was a tear and the van had been ripped wide open on the other side, it sank.

The chant of a woman selling oranges, her back to the pier, "Five-five kobo; five-five—" was suddenly loud and sharp. She broke off, startled by the sound of her own voice. And then the stunned crowd broke loose. They shouted and laughed, whistled and stomped. Some of the men danced, and the trunks of the palm trees came alive with boys shinnying up for a better look. I knew without turning that hundreds more were running down the hill from their huts, and the noise would get louder.

Boxes began to pop up in the water by the edge of the freighter, two or three suitcases, and what looked like a large wooden mask, books, pillows, cushions, and odds and ends I couldn't make out. Fifty or sixty boys, naked or in shorts, dove from the bank and swam toward the things, setting off another uproar.

Just as the van fell free from the sling, the man watching on the pier had raised his hand as if to stop it, to give some signal that would reverse the catastrophe. His hand remained there after the van sank. He lowered it when the shouting began behind him, glancing back as if it were the cause of all the hilarity. The woman scarcely moved; her arms stiffened at her sides, I thought, and she clenched her fists, but she didn't look back. They had been standing a bit apart. When the boys began diving into the river, the man stepped closer to her to say something. I had the feeling, I didn't know why, that he was smiling or even laughing as he spoke. Her face was tilted toward his; she wore glasses. As he spoke his hands moved not in agitation but slowly, opening and closing as if he were explaining something. She seemed not to say anything, but she kept glancing at the things in the water as if to connect them with what he was saying. I had a feeling, I don't know why, something about the set of their shoulders maybe, that neither of them was interested in rescuing the things that could be saved. Suddenly, after listening to him for half a minute or so, the woman swung a roundhouse right at him. He jerked back enough that she missed his jaw and hit his shoulder. The mob around the pier, now five or six hundred strong, broke into fresh laughter. I felt embarrassed, as if I had been caught eavesdropping on them, but I began to work my way around the edge of the crowd, intending to go offer them my help.

The boys had reached the things floating in the water. They paid no attention to the security guards yelling on the pier. They grabbed whatever they could and fled with it toward the riverbank. One had the transparent top to a record player, another waved a hiking boot over his head. One struggled with a rolling pin and several kitchen cannisters. Half a dozen tugged at a suitcase until it burst open. They fought over the clothing in it, pulling underwear over their heads and arms. Two of them swam back together, each clutching half of the suitcase. One boy swam to the pier with what I had taken to be a mask—it was—and appeared to be bargaining with the couple for a reward.

Before I reached the pier I saw Harry McIvor's broad shoulders and square head pumping up and down as he pushed in the same direction. Gwen McIvor, her shoulders nearly as broad as his, was with him. I stopped, knowing the newcomers were in good hands and, to tell the truth, not anxious to meet them just then. Some of the things I had seen spill into the water, the cushions, potted plants, even the kitchenware and television, were not what people brought to Harbourworks. You came to Harbourworks to trade a piece of time from your life—a year or two years, sometimes ten or twenty, like Gwen and Harry McIvor. You traded it for money to make things better or ends meet back home, maybe even to live in luxury, but one thing was always clear: back home *was* home, and Harbourworks was not. I had the feeling these people didn't do it that way, that what was in that van was everything they owned. I had the feeling I had just seen their home go down in eighty feet of water, and in the little scene on the pier, maybe more go down than that.

In the meantime, I needed sleep. I went back to my duplex and got it.

II

I met the Ransoms that evening at the McIvors'. All the talk, of course, was about their loss—clothing, stereo, tapes, television, voltage converters, tools, tableware, books, carvings from Sierra Leone, masks from Senegal, brass trays from Morocco, bicycles—the list lengthened as Danny and Marty turned from one new face to another. The van broke open "like a sack of candy," I heard Danny say, and then others repeating it.

What Danny thought right then was, he said, that he wanted to be someone else.

"I'd noticed a skinny kid behind us," he said; "he was sleeping. There was a big fly, tsetse fly for all he cared, on his nose, and he never twitched. But after the van fell he ran around like a madman, turning cartwheels. That's what I thought after the damned thing went under: I wish I was that kid."

Most of the people on Harry and Gwen McIvor's veranda that evening, I was pretty sure, were embarrassed, not at Danny's attitude toward their loss, or Marty's either, for they were hitting just the right Harbourworks tone: we lost something; so what? Everyone loses something. Let's get on with it. But Danny talked with a lot of animation—eyebrows arching and falling, mobile jaw, lively Adam's apple, mouth opening wide, lively blue eyes searching you out, insisting that you laugh with him and see the boy doing cartwheels. He was good-looking enough, mid thirties, skinny with the beginnings of a paunch, broad smile; but he wanted you to know more than most Harbourworks people were used to knowing. I could see some of the others squirming, even as they filled themselves in on every detail of the little catastrophe—it wasn't the first, wouldn't be the last—at Mbopo Pier.

For a while, compared to Danny, Marty Ransom seemed mousy to me that first Sunday evening. Huddled in one of Gwen McIvor's huge, shapeless dresses between Gwen and Harry along the half-wall of their screened veranda, legs folded under her, she seemed small, almost pinch-faced, her light-brown hair cut very short, not so much smiling as smirking when Danny and the rest of us laughed. I winced when she occasionally broke into Danny's long story; her voice sounded like it was coming over the telephone, or from one of those talking dolls my daughters had wanted for

Christmas. But as the beer loosened us up—including Bob Mullin, who was off in a corner, sitting very sheepishly under his thick head bandage—and we all trotted out our own disasters, I began to like her quick movements when she looked from one speaker to another, her smirk and snicker when, his massive pipe clamped in his long, sun-reddened jaw, Harry bent over her to tell one of his stale jokes in a raspy, growling voice.

"American? You're too big not to have played football," Danny said to me when Harry introduced us. "College? Pro?"

"High school, and not much of that," I said.

"Why are the chairs lined up along the walls?" he asked a little too loudly. "Like the bloody army?"

"Nigerian custom. We can't seem to break it." I was glad Gwen and Harry were out of earshot. Danny's "bloody" didn't fit: we Americans never got that word just right.

Danny's brows arched. "More likely the British taught them. It strikes me as more Anglo-Saxon than Efik."

I glanced around. Most of us at Harbourworks didn't bother to know the name of the largest tribe in the area.

"Great beer." He held up a green Champion bottle. "We learned that ten years ago when we came down through Maiduguri from Lake Chad."

"You drove from Maiduguri?" I asked, remembering that he had tried to drive from Sierra Leone.

"They held us up two days at the border." He laughed, his brows arching again. "So which is your wife? Or are you one of the two bachelors?"

"Two?" I pushed my glasses down my nose and looked around: Bob and I were the only single men. "How'd you know?"

"Sixteen of us, nine men and seven women. The Brits—the women I mean—can't count except in twos. So there are seven couples and two bachelors."

We were separated as Nick and Betty Allan pushed in, eager to be the first to pass along all the essential information: there's no fresh milk and only canned cheese; the cigarette venders will try to sell you Nigerian-made Benson and Hedges for British; if you run over someone in your car, drive on, and if you can't drive, get out and run, because the villagers will chop you to pieces with their matchets; every public official wants "kola," a bribe, so let Harbourworks do your paperwork for you because they bribe at the top and that takes care of the lot; the telephone system is useless, but sometimes you can call home from our supply ships; the beer is made in a German-run brewery and is very good, but you have to own a case of empty bottles before you can buy it, and bottles are worth their weight in gold; small loss your television—the only channel here is all local politics; was it an American-made van? If it was, it'd have been a pile of rust in a year anyway; boil and filter your water yourself; watch your steward when he disinfects your fruits and vegetables; keep your whisky under lock and key . . . all the things we'd been told when we came, until others arrived and we could repeat them as if they were our personal discoveries. The Ransoms probably knew this—Danny said that, besides Sierra Leone, they had done a stint in Senegal, and Peace Corps time in Chad—but we weren't going to let them escape the ritual.

Everyone was recuperating from the Barnsdalls' party. The tennis players—Nick and Betty Allan, Colin Deaver, Kumar, even Gabe Barnsdall—had sweated out some of the night's sin, and I had been down at the pier, but the rest were eating and drinking their hangovers away and reconstructing the party with mock penitence. It occurred to me that the Ransoms would have been better off if I hadn't gone to the pier.

"My name is Howard Westfall. Sorry about your things," I said when it was my turn to talk to Marty Ransom. "You must be fed up with hearing that by now."

"People need to show they care, don't they?" Her teeth were crooked, her eyes enlarged behind glasses in small square frames, her breasts small, her voice edged with that electronic hollowness.

"It wouldn't have happened if Bob Mullin had been on the job. He's the crane operator—" I nodded toward Bob—"in the mummy getup over there. But he banged his head on the bottom of the swimming pool early this morning."

She laughed. "We'll sue him when he recovers. If he recovers."

I repeated what she had probably heard many times already, especially from the Irish. "He's Irish; it's the pool we're worried about. Actually, I'm partly to blame. I didn't realize he was going to dive in at the wrong end until too late."

"Oh, you were there."

"I was there."

"So we can sue you both."

"Might as well; we've been in jams together before. We met on a rig in the North Sea. Bob got me my job here, in fact. He'll be around to apologize. I'm sorry for my part too."

"We're used to losing things. It's like freedom, isn't it? Being free of what we collect? Danny said that, I think."

I wondered if that was what he'd been saying when she hit him at the pier. Danny's voice carried across the veranda, loud and happy. Gabe and Sheila Barnsdall were listening to him, looking more interested than usual for a Sunday evening, but not quite comfortable.

I pointed across the backyard at some villagers watching us through the chain-link fence topped with concertina wire that surrounded the compound. "How about them? They own the lappas they're wearing and maybe a short-handled hoe. Are they freer than we are?"

"They're outside the fence. Don't you wish you were sometimes?"

"Well—" I wasn't sure if she was laughing with me or at me.

"Did you hear what Danny said about wanting to be someone else?" she asked. "He meant it. Isn't that why everybody is here? To be someone else? To get outside the fence? Otherwise they'd stay home in Ireland, or Pennsylvania."

"I saw the accident this morning," I said. I hadn't meant to tell her, certainly not to blurt it out.

"You were there?"

"I'm a mechanic. I was called down to start the crane engine."

"You seem to be everywhere." She eyed me thoughtfully. "So you saw everything."

"I really felt bad about it."

"Everything," she repeated.

I had the feeling she was moving inside Gwen McIvor's huge dress the way women sometimes moved at our parties late at night when they'd had a lot to drink. Suddenly her small, smirking mouth with its dab of lipstick—Gwen's, probably—seemed very generous.

"Are you from Pennsylvania?" I asked.

"Philadelphia. Danny's from Cleveland." She glanced at Bob Mullin, whose dome of bandages was bobbing little more than shoulder-high to the other men as he crossed the room to join us. She said to me, "You're one of the bachelors, aren't you?"

"How'd you know?"

She moved—definitely—inside the dress. "Any woman could tell. You . . . look a lot. What's your wife's name? Where are you from?"

"Austin. Texas. Her name is Linda. She and the girls were here once. They lasted ten days. In fact, I had trouble getting her to come out here from the airport."

"Do you write her?"

"Every other Sunday. Never miss."

"Poor men," she said; "Mrs. McIvor says there are a hundred men and less than thirty women."

"Right."

"You must suffer so much—" her eyelids, slightly enlarged through her glasses, batted rapidly, and I knew she was laughing at me—"with no . . . outlet."

"We do." I tried to follow her lead and put on a woeful face. She was on uncertain ground. Harbourworks women generally pretended to ignore our forays among the whores at the Luna Bar in Georgetown, or showed grim toleration at most. It depended on whether we brought the girls back to the compound, how openly, how often, and how long we kept them here. But the gossip about who queued up at Kumar's clinic the following week for penicillin shots was loud and malicious.

"And the wives mistreat you—make you run all sorts of errands before they'll ask you to dinner, like tonight?"

I said, "Well . . . yes, as a matter of fact." Despite another hangover, I'd been at the Georgetown beach at sunup the day before, Saturday, because Gwen McIvor had wanted fresh shrimp from a Spanish trawler. Harry was on duty on the dredge, she'd said, but I saw him coming in with the golfers around noon. Some of the wives put up with our need to talk and dance with them and perhaps steal a kiss, or even let a hand wander too far in the wee drunken hours of Saturday or Sunday morning. But most of them seemed continually exasperated that our own wives weren't there, to lighten their social burdens, I suppose, the compound-wide Friday and Saturday night parties that fell to each married couple's lot every three months, the Sunday curry brunches and evening recovery parties, weekday dinners.

"All the time," Bob broke in. "They treat us worse than Nigerian chickens, these wives treat us."

"I like your beard, Howard." Marty gave me a last smile and touched my arm lightly as she turned to Bob.

"What about *my* beard?" he asked.

The McIvors' steward was serving the chicken curry at the buffet table. I took a plate and got in line more quickly than usual. Marty's questions had brought back the time Linda and the girls had been here. Linda—and Melody and Cindy too—had hated it: the touts pressing in on them at the airport; the customs inspector who had opened all their bags and scattered their clothing up and down the counter; the mounds of garbage on the streets being foraged by goats, chickens, dogs, and children; the heat and creeping, honking traffic of Georgetown. Linda had hated the African sky, its humid dome so close you sometimes felt you could touch the curve of it; it choked her, she said. She hated being watched by the villagers outside the fence. She hated the English wives' dropped *r*'s, hated what she called the "gobble-gobble" of mixed accents at the first, and only, weekend party we went to, although she had, I thought, enjoyed herself at the beginning, even when Archibald Ekong, the Indigenous Director, moved in quickly to dance with her. I was nervous about that; her experience was limited to the little all-white town near the Red River where we had grown up and after that to Austin, so he was probably the first black she had ever touched. But that went all right. Then, however, some man had slapped her across the buttocks. She had strode over to where I was singing a ballad with Harry McIvor and Kumar and said she wanted to leave. I tried to laugh it off, saying the wrong thing, "It doesn't mean much here; you shouldn't take it seriously." I followed her out on the street, but before I could get her into my duplex and promise to arrange their return tickets the next day, she screamed, "You're just little white men playing God in the middle of all these niggers! Is this what you need to feel important?"

So my family had gone home, and after that I went to the Luna Bar with a clear conscience. I had made an honest effort for things to be otherwise.

The curried chicken was bland by Texas standards. The British have a way of making all food taste boiled. Bob and Marty were across the room. He was laughing, shaking his turbaned head. She curved her hands beneath her breasts, then held them flatly over her groin to shape something, I couldn't tell what. I made my apologies to Gwen, went to the quarters, and roused out Paul to drive me to the Luna, even if tomorrow was a working day. He didn't dare complain because he knew I'd been looking for him that morning.

At the Luna I ordered two beers, one for me and one for Bassey, who was pleased to see me, or any customer, I was sure, on a Sunday evening. She was a short, sturdy young woman with oiled, harshly straightened hair, large, perfectly white teeth, and a rich laugh. She didn't object when I left the beer, which was warm. She seldom drank anyway. Paul drove us back to Harbourworks. In my bedroom we undressed briskly. She aligned herself to me under the sheets in the chill of the air conditioner and, finding me already erect, said "Ah!" in pleased surprise.

Afterward she snuggled against me, using my arm as a pillow, and giggled. "This big man Howard is youngman tonight."

We had a few things we could talk about. She asked after my daughters, and my wife. She told me her children were well and that the yam harvest in her village had been good. Then, when we usually dozed off, I reached for her again. I didn't let myself wonder until later, after I had awakened Paul in the Land Cruiser to drive her back to town, what a slender woman with small breasts and glasses, a smirk, and a voice that sounded like a tape played too fast had to do with my extra energy.

III

Despite their unpleasant arrival, the Ransoms settled into Harbourworks so easily that the veterans were suspicious. By Tuesday we heard that Danny had found a reliable source of fresh eggs at a good price and that four crates of Champion beer were locked in the Ransoms' pantry, and by Wednesday that their steward—furnished by Harbourworks, of course—had served an enormous baked freshwater fish for dinner.

"I was here six blooming weeks before I got a crate of bottles," Bob Mullin said at the Harbourworks bar Tuesday night. "And two of them was cracked." Kumar had reduced Bob's bandages to a broad patch covering his forehead from temple to temple. Monday Obuku had been sacked.

"Betty says Asuquo wastes a day a week looking for eggs," Nick Allan added.

"Lovely bird, Danny's wife," Bob said.

On Wednesday night at the bar Harry McIvor said, "Danny's got the switchboard set to rights. Never worked before, not once in ten years."

"He's good with the wires," Nick said.

"Now my problem is keeping the other bastards from stealing him," Harry said. "Jamie Stevenson was after him today."

On Monday I had watched Danny open and tackle the switchboard. When the big engines were humming properly, I watched other people work or picked up one of the half-dozen novels I was reading simultaneously. He had laughed out loud when he saw that some of the wires were rope-thick with fungus, and his brows had danced. He worked straight through lunch, whistling and talking to himself, and looked up in surprise when Harry stopped him at five-thirty.

Danny himself came in then, so Harry broke off his praises.

"I heard you had fresh fish tonight," I said. "All the wives will be groveling at your feet. Their stewards come back with stockfish, full of worms."

He grinned and offered me a cigarette from the first pack of Rothmans I had seen in three months. "You want fresh fish, go where they catch fresh fish. We drove into a little fishing village upriver yesterday just as the canoes came in."

Danny had also commandeered one of the Harbourworks Land Cruisers, always in short supply, in record time. I said, "Speaking of driving—"

"Use a Harbourworks driver? So if I have a wreck it's his fault and the natives can tear him to pieces?"

"Right. It happened two years ago in Ekpo Abasi, that village this side of the police checkpoint. Except the driver had sense enough to run and Billy Reneau didn't. There wasn't much left of him."

Danny nodded. "Harry told me. I feel like an idiot having someone else drive for me."

"Better to feel like an idiot."

Marty joined us then, trim and un-mousy in a tie-dye dress of coarse cotton. She said it was from Onwuchekwa Market in town, where the Harbourworks wives seldom ventured. It had slits up each thigh.

Two bottles of Champion later, Danny began to talk about Harbourworks. "It's your basic adult playpen. Golf course, tennis courts, swimming pool, a bar with cheap booze, servants, night watchmen, drivers, air-conditioned houses bigger than most of us have ever lived in, or will live in again—especially the Brits. Do you have any idea the sort of housing most of these Brits were used to back home? Take a crane operator like Bob Mullin—"

"Danny, shut up," Marty said. Bob was in the bar, across the room, but the stereo was loud enough that he couldn't hear.

"But the Brits have class," Danny resumed after a minute or so. "Americans don't know what to do with servants. We make them sit down and have a beer with us one minute, then kick them like dogs the next. The

Brits would never have a beer with them, but they wouldn't kick them either. In Sierra Leone a guy we knew from Indiana made his houseboy bring his wife in to have a drink with them at the dining table, the three of them. Pregnant, mind you. Then he—"

"Danny, shut up," Marty said again, with no apparent anger.

Danny was a reader too. We discovered a mutual love for Fowles' *Daniel Martin*, but disgust for *Maggot*. Danny had read Sean O'Casey too. Bob, although he wasn't a reader himself, had given me a collection of O'Casey's plays.

Later on Bob joined us, and at closing time Danny invited him and me to their house for a nightcap, which we declined. Then he asked us to dinner the following evening, and when Marty seconded the invitation, we accepted.

One of the engines on the dredge went down the next morning. It was nearly dark before I had it back together and running. By the time I had showered, dressed, and bullied Okpara, the Harbourworks bartender, out of a bottle of good wine for the Ransoms I arrived late at their house, which was three lanes over from my duplex in Bachelors' Quarters.

Bob had been there for some time, I judged, by the flush of his dark face under his black, square, smoothly trimmed beard and by the way his eyes followed Marty. The Ransoms were wearing matching lappas, bright yellow with black and green puddles of color in them. Their steward, Akpan, chuckled every time he looked at them. Danny had mastered the huge knot the village men used to hold their lappas at the waist, but the fold of Marty's lappa over her breasts loosened every few minutes, causing a little crisis of giggling and clutching. Finally she went to the bedroom and returned with the cloth safety-pinned.

I could feel Akpan's uneasy eyes on Bob and me as he served dinner. He had been a Harbourworks steward for many years—the last six with Lloyd Davison, the assistant superintendent, until Lloyd's retirement—and I was sure he had as firm a notion of what expatriates ate, and should eat, as any Englishman. Nevertheless, what he brought to the table was a large bowl of small cone-shaped snails, periwinkles, in a thick red sauce; pounded yam, white and fluffy; a dark, strong-smelling, steaming mass that I thought might be bitterleaf; and a fresh fruit dish in which I recognized pawpaw, coconut, and perhaps soursop, but nothing else.

"Sir," Akpan said apprehensively to Bob as the periwinkles dropped like stones onto his plate, "Master says make this native soup. He says he wants it—"

Danny laughed. "We had a long discussion with Akpan. We tried to convince him we're not interested in roast beef or Yorkshire pudding."

The tips of the snail shells had been broken off, and Danny showed us how to suck out the meat while Akpan hovered over us, clucking anxiously and then grinning as we began to nod and say we liked them, and to prove it by the growing mound of finished shells in the center of the table. He laughed aloud when Danny and Marty, and then Bob and I too, rolled balls of the pounded yam with our fingers, dipped them in the hot pepper sauce, and ate them.

We drank the bottle of wine I had brought, another and then another that Danny had, he assured us, got at a good price in town. Sweat ran down my face, and Bob's too, produced by the fiery periwinkle soup and an even hotter mango pickle, Indian-made. I tried to eat the strong-smelling stuff—it was a little like spinach—and gave up. Bob didn't try. Danny had repaired, and claimed, a broken stereo that Lloyd Davison had left behind. Danny said something about Nigerian reggae coming from Jamaica. Marty disagreed with him, and the argument evolved into a laughing, hip-shoving match at the stereo, with Bob and me egging on and refereeing. It reminded me of the swing Marty had taken at Danny on the pier. Marty won, and the elastic beat of one of Lagos's many-wived stars filled the room.

Bob told how he and I had become friends, an incident known as the Battle of Aberdeen. Because, he said, I had parked in the wrong place, he swung a load of sucker rod into the pickup I had just vacated, shearing the cab off. A week later I spotted him in a bar in Aberdeen and called him a "midget terrorist." In the "fight" that followed, I held him off with my eight-inch reach advantage and laughed while he fanned the air. He finally suggested I ought to buy him a pint, since he had done all the fighting and was too winded to order.

I told my story of seeing the van drop at Mbopo Pier, dwelling on the loafers' hilarity along the bank and the boys swimming out to grab Danny and Marty's things. I could feel Marty's eyes on me, and I said nothing about her hitting Danny. When I finished, she smiled at me, and her bare feet rested on mine.

The wine settled in, Marty's freckled shoulders glistened in the candle-light, and her quick eyes caught the candle flames—no trick at all to find candles, Danny said. He brought out a kola nut and broke it open while Akpan nodded approvingly.

"Good custom this," Danny said. "Only friends can spread their mats in your hut and share a kola nut."

I felt the quick jolt of caffeine as we chewed on the nut. Danny launched into a laughing, mocking summation of the Harbourworks mission. "We dig out the bottom of this bloody bend in the river and make mountains with the silt where a hundred villagers used to have yam plots; next rainy season the river silts up the hole we dug, and we dig it out again; we bribe the right people in the military dictatorship, and everybody at the top's happy and will be happy till the price of oil drops; then the country will be bankrupt, we'll go home to enjoy all the Nigerian dollars we've socked away, all the crooks we've been bribing will go to Switzerland where *they've* been socking away dollars, the Nigerians won't have any more harbor when we leave than when the first shrewd son of a bitch talked them into doing it in the first place, and the villagers can eat the weeds on these damned mountains of silt we've left them." While he talked Marty said "Shut up, Danny" now and then and fiddled with her safety pins.

"We're gaining on it." Bob turned his wineglass slowly in the flame of the candle. "They could dock an aircraft carrier here, come next year."

"If they had one," I said.

Danny and Bob strayed into a discussion of Mammy Wata, the goddess of the river, and what Danny called "parallel causality with circular pre-punishment." The gist of it was, I gathered as under the table Marty's feet pushed my sandals off and layered themselves between mine, that Mammy Wata, seeing that Bob was about to cause the Ransoms' van to sink in eighty feet of water by cracking his skull against the bottom of the swimming pool and thereby leaving Monday Obuku in charge of the crane—that the goddess, divining that he was going to do it anyway—*caused* him to dive into the shallow end of the pool and have a near-concussion as punishment for doing it. The parallel events—the van's dive, Bob's dive—were, Danny explained, "A sublime example of the goddess's weakness for cosmic symmetry."

"It's all bloody gravity anyway," he said. "All loss is caused by gravity. Your bloody goddesses would be nowhere without it."

When, somewhere in the philosophical mire, Bob mentioned that Monday Obuku had been fired, Marty untangled our feet long enough to grasp his thickly-haired arm and plead for Monday's reinstatement, which Bob agreed to attempt. Around midnight, Bob and I walked silently back to the Bachelors' Quarters. There was no need to tell each other it was the most pleasant evening we'd ever spent in Harbourworks.

IV

As Harry McIvor had feared, Jamie Stevenson and the other section chiefs did kidnap Danny to help them with their electrical equipment, some of which had remained crated for months or even years because no one knew what to do with it. When the section chiefs weren't after him, he often spent an evening or a Saturday finding, for a desperate hostess, fresh fish, a hindquarter of Fulani beef, melons from Kano, or even, somehow, croissants and long loaves of French bread from Douala, across the border in Cameroun. And he started a garden behind his house, breaking into the leached soil with a hoe while amused villagers crowded the fence to watch and Akpan shook his head.

Still, he got to the bar most weeknights at least by nine o'clock, and here it was at the big center table that Bob and I, and sometimes others too, but always Bob and I, talked with Danny past closing time, until the sleepy Okpara chased us out with his twig broom. Or we listened to him, his brows arching wildly, arms flailing, as he unraveled tales of disaster and near-disaster while crossing the Sahara with Marty ("in a bloody Plymouth station wagon, mind you, here we are trying to dig ourselves out of sand over the axles; we see these bloody Frenchmen coming and think we're saved, and they sail past us without so much as giving us the finger; two days later we throw out our clothes and suitcases and bronze heads and ebony carvings from Benin City to lighten the car; next day we throw out three of our last four jerry cans of water and half our petrol; then we discover our last can of water has been leaking, and we don't have the foggiest how far we are from El Golea"); of Marty losing her passport on the way to Timbuktu by bush taxi, boat, and donkey, somewhere between the boat and donkey; of sleeping with Arabs on a narrow road in Mali and awakening to find their shoes stolen; of Danny, but not Marty, vomiting when they learned they had eaten cane rat in a pepper soup near Onitsha— endless tales, less fascinating in themselves than in the wonder with which Danny told them, the surprise with which he saw the Danny of his stories having his pockets picked in Chad as he pushed a bag atop a bus rack, or awakening in Senegal in time to see his pants float across the bedroom on a hooked stick:

"I thought I was dreaming; I sat up in bed naked as a baby and watched my only pair of jeans disappear through a hole they'd cut in the window screen."

Sometimes Kumar came in around ten o'clock for half an hour and a single weak scotch and water, after he had completed his "second shift," when he treated, for cash only, a long line of Nigerians, many of them from Archibald Ekong's enormous extended family. His second shift, according to Harry, created Kumar's only problem: "How to convert shoeboxes full of naira into shoeboxes full of dollars and get them out of the country." Some of Kumar's Indian compatriots solved the problem for him. What Kumar did was also illegal, but—Harry would shift his pipe from one side of his mouth to the other and say—"for Harbourworks, absolute political expediency."

When Kumar joined us, Danny asked questions and talked less, for Kumar had been there longer than anyone else except Harry, and he knew far more Nigerians than Harry. He could speak the local pidgin fluently. Short, trim, almost baby-faced, he answered some of Danny's questions and laughed off the rest, saying, "Why do you want to know so much? You are healthy, the beer is good, you are making money. That's enough."

At the weekend parties, Danny became a fixture at the bar—Harbour-works had a portable bar in four sections that was moved from house to house—talking, talking with the slowly milling population of the compound. He was the recipient, after a few weeks, of a parade of kisses and embraces from the wives. They put some zing in our Harbourworks lives, Marty in her Nigerian outfits and Danny with his blasphemous talk about the injustices and outright theft we expatriates were guilty of. Some people looked around nervously, especially if Archibald Ekong was there; but once they understood it was just talk they welcomed it, I suppose, as another version of the cynicism we all felt anyway. I admired Danny because he had done things I would have loved to say I'd done—crossed the Sahara, gone to Timbuktu, lived through a locust infestation in Chad. He had taken risks, he and Marty. I had seen things too—six armed robbers tied to posts and machine-gunned in Onitsha one rainy Saturday afternoon, one military dictatorship overturned by another—but I had slept in my own bed in Harbourworks the same night, and the Harbourworks generators had kept my air conditioners blowing steadily.

Bob had got Monday Obuku's job back for him. His bandages grew smaller until he was left with a thoroughly scabbed forehead. He and I were usually there with Danny, unless Marty tugged one of us off to the dance floor. Around midnight Danny became the bartender, still talking but efficient, able to serve up any drink you could name so long as the ingredients were available, and there he remained, apparently no less sober than when he had arrived, until the last, most determined and besotted drunk of the party sagged to the floor and passed out. Often he locked up the house for the hosts, long since in bed, and awakened Marty from one of the couches.

Bob and I had dinner at the Ransoms' house at least twice a week. Others came too, the McIvors or Barnsdalls or Allans, sometimes someone from town that we had never seen in Harbourworks—an Egyptian gynecologist, the captain and first mate of the Spanish trawler, a hard-drinking Jesuit priest from Zimbabwe—and a steady flow of Nigerians: contractors, an agricultural advisor, an herbal doctor, even a small, spidery Ibibio palm-wine tapper for whom Akpan refused to serve as translator. Bob and I did our best to reciprocate the Ransoms' hospitality, bringing shrimp from the trawler, fresh goat meat, beef, whisky, and wine when we could find it. Occasionally we treated them to the high-priced bad food at the Federal Hotel in town, or to an even more expensive Lebanese restaurant where only those on expense accounts could afford to eat regularly.

Marty made it far from easy on me. The nudging of her knee or stroking of her bare feet under the table continued, and there were quick smiling kisses just beyond the dining room door, glimpses of freckled shoulders or the crescent of a small soft breast, of a thigh flashing unexpectedly from an innocent-looking skirt.

At the parties she was usually out on the veranda dancing—all the houses were built on the same plan, and the veranda had become by common consent the dance floor. She was almost never with Danny, unless it was early in the evening. Danny preferred the bar. She danced with husbands and bachelors alike, summoning Bob or me away from Danny if she ran out of partners. The women liked her, I think partly because of her odd doll-voice, which was no threat, and partly because by tugging the men indiscriminately to their feet she got them to stay up a while and quicken the pace of the party, instead of sinking into their weekend exhaustion or booze, or both.

It was pleasure, and pain, for me to feel the agile, girlish movements of Marty's limbs and the sudden frankness of her hips, to want her. An odd effect of my friendship with her and Danny was that, around eleven at the Friday night parties, and sometimes Saturday night too, I left more and more often to drive into Georgetown to the Luna Bar. There, from among the whores who crowded the tables, I selected one of the girls with "safe" reputations—Bassey, if she was available, or Felicity, Nfim, Anna—and brought her back to my duplex. Bob too sometimes took leave with a wink and some comment about obligations in town. But I didn't see him at the Luna or meet him around sunup as I was taking Bassey, or Felicity, whomever, home to her shack on one of the narrow, tortuous lanes on the hill above Mbopo Pier.

On a Friday night in late February, rain was pattering lightly on the corrugated metal roof of the Stevensons' house. It was the first break in the dry season. Marty had been dancing with the Indigenous Director, Archibald Ekong, who, although he was as tall and heavy as I, was as light on his feet on the dance floor as he was smart and quick on the tennis court. One of his wives, or girl friends, a tall, haughty young woman with skin much lighter than his and an elaborate, corral-like hairdo that must have taken a full day to sculpture, had sat stiffly on a chair against the wall while Archibald danced. At last he came from the veranda, said his good-byes, and the woman followed him out the door, where his driver was waiting with an umbrella.

At the bar, Danny had organized a "blind drunk" conversation, with all of the barflies holding beercaps wedged like monocles over both eyes. Then a long story of Danny's about crocodiles attacking road construction workers in Dahomey had turned into a noisy debate about the land speed of a hungry twenty-foot crocodile. I was edging away from the debate and the bar, intending to drive into town, when Marty caught my arm and pulled me toward the veranda.

"I have to leave," I protested.

"One dance." She was wearing a heavy, striped dress with a foil-like sheen, popular with the wealthier Efik women in Georgetown. It draped from her shoulders in complicated, voluminous folds to the floor.

"Where are you going?" she asked when we were on the veranda, tucking herself against me.

"Early call on the dredge tomorrow."

"Liar. You're going to the Luna."

When I didn't answer, she said, "Aren't you afraid you'll catch something?"

"Don't know what you're talking about, Lady."

"Stop it." Her doll-voice had an edge to it. "Is she good?"

I grinned. "Like I said, Lady, don't—"

She guided my hand through the intricate folds of her dress to the moist skin over her ribs and her small, soft breast. "You can save yourself a trip tonight."

Our deception of Danny—my goodnight shout as I passed the bar, Danny's wave and Bob's wink and enjoinder to "give them my love," Marty's exit ten minutes later out the veranda door, her quick step on the wet gravel before my unlighted porch, her last glance back down the lane, our embrace behind the closed door—was calm, our undressing and placing of our glasses next to a letter from Linda on the nightstand matter-of-fact, our fumbling amiable. After my surprise at touching hair not tied up in stubby braids or greased in poor imitation of Western fashions, at Marty's rougher, warmer, and slacker skin, at being met with open-mouthed kisses instead of the wary peck-pecking of the Luna whores, our lovemaking was leisurely, and even humorous. As I smoothed Marty's short, frizzy hair and she worked her feet between mine while we rested after our joining, I remember feeling, in my lack of any sense of furtiveness or fear that Danny would burst through the door, something almost like disappointment.

"Tell me what you really saw at Mbopo Pier," she demanded.

I knew what she meant. "After the van fell, Danny seemed to be explaining something to you."

"He was talking rubbish about us being washed clean of our sins by losing all our possessions. He tried to make it a religious joke."

"So you slugged him."

She hid her face against my chest. "The son of a bitch was talking like that when he should have been crying, or hugging me."

The music pounded loudly at the Stevensons' house a few hundred yards away—I had turned off the air conditioner and opened the jalousies—coming to us clearly through the breezeless air and reverberating against the concrete walls of my bedroom. In the bush beyond the chain-link fence a big drum boomed, and we could hear the sharp chanting of a woman, then an answering chorus from the dancers. The rain still pattered finely behind the louder dripping from the tin roof. Marty lay with her head on my chest, her short hair tickling my chin, my hand at the bone and swell of her hip. We were sweating in the warm night, the clinging sheet kicked to the foot of the bed.

"I hated pretending it didn't matter that first night at the McIvors'," she said. "Why would we pack our things in the first place if it didn't matter?"

"Everything is temporary here. If something went wrong we'd leave it all. We'd leave naked if we had to." I stretched until the joints in my ankles crackled, wanting her to be quiet and go to sleep where she was, wanting her to leave so I could sleep. I thought of Danny. He would be behind the bar by now, serving drinks and talk.

Marty said, "I can't think how many friends we've had and lost in Africa. We say we'll meet here or there or do this or that, but we never do."

She nuzzled my beard and turned my face to hers. "We're temporary too. So this is important. It's important to kiss."

Later she said, "Tell me about Texas." So I told her about growing up in Foraker near the Red River, about my father teaching me, when I hadn't hidden out with a book, how to use acetylene and electric welders and how to repair any kind of machine that came through the door of his shop on the edge of town, which was half garage, half smithy, and all grease and mounds of rusting engine parts. And—why, I don't know—I told her about my best friend, Phil Mac Rettinger, screaming on the football field one night when we were juniors, his leg bent the wrong way, about my dropping my helmet, saying "I don't need this," and getting into the ambulance with him, about how the whole town, at least it seemed so then, including my father and Phil Mac, had called me a quitter, but I refused to play again. Phil Mac had never walked properly after that.

Marty asked, "Is that a letter from your wife?"

"Yes. It came today."

"Does she say she loves you?"

The question irritated me. Our letters, Linda's and mine, had settled into our concerns: the girls and their school, interest rates, house taxes, problems with cars or plumbing (Linda's letters) or machinery (mine). I asked, "How do old married couples write about love? Do they say it's up half a point, or down? Cindy's getting a retainer. Melody's hair is turning darker. That's what we write about."

"Grouch," she said.

She turned her back to me and rested her head on my arm. Her doll-like voice seemed to come from the other side of the room. "I had an old cotton blouse in the van. I started to throw it away, but I put it in the glove compartment instead. I'd had it since I was twelve."

She began to cry. "It was just an old blouse. All faded out."

She cried for a long time, so quietly that I knew she was still awake only by an occasional low sob, while I stroked her shoulder drowsily. Finally the numbness in my arm grew painful and I had to move it.

Before she got up to dress she turned, the tears gone and the crooked smile in place, and said, "You do love me, don't you?"

I answered after a moment, "Yes, I do."

She swung her feet off the bed, took her glasses with their small, square frames from the nightstand, and put them on. Then she leaned over me, still smiling. "More than Danny?"

V

I didn't know if anyone had seen or suspected us that Friday night, and I didn't expect to; Harbourworks gossip operated according to strict rules, one of them being that the principals were never exposed to it. Marty returned to the Stevensons' house before three, went back through the veranda door, found a dancing partner, and didn't check to see, she told me later, if Danny was still at the bar until around four, when people began to leave.

She came to my duplex once each of the next four weekends from the parties and several times on weeknights while Danny was at the Harbourworks bar. If anything, she was more open with her kisses and touches after that night than before, and less tolerant of Danny's long tirades and longer tales. I was at their house nearly every evening, along with Bob. In the mornings I crawled out of bed dehydrated, my head pounding at a rate unusual even for Harbourworks.

One morning on the dredge after a late night at the bar, not with Marty, I overturned two cups of coffee in succession. Harry McIvor tapped me on the shoulder and said, "Burning it a bit, aren't we?" and I knew I had to break the pattern. I began to skip some of the bar sessions and—more difficult—sometimes dinner with Marty and Danny.

"I'm going to cave in if I don't drink less and get more sleep," I explained at the Ransoms' house. "You understand I enjoy it. Other than this ugly Irishman Mullin you two are the best thing that's happened to me in Harbourworks. I just—"

"Old age is a 'orrible thing, ain't it?" Bob said.

Danny grinned. "What are you apologizing about? Nothing's going to change; we'll just do a little less of it."

Marty came around the table and kissed me on the mouth. "Listen to Danny, Howard; he knows you still love us."

Which was true. But in the next few weeks when I heard Marty's step on my dark porch, I also began to hear, louder and louder, her question: "More than Danny? More than Danny?" I began to see him on the wall of my bedroom over her shoulder, his lively eyebrows and flailing arms, talking away; then a night came when he stopped talking and just looked at me, and I knew another pattern had to be broken.

"I can't do this," I said.

Marty sat up cross-legged on the bed. "I can see you can't. What's wrong, Love?"

"I keep seeing Danny. As clear—"

She slapped me, a solid swat that made my head ring, its echo bouncing off the concrete walls like a squash ball. Then she put on her glasses and began to dress.

"What was that about?" I asked.

"Sorry. Women do overreact when their lovers disappoint them, don't they?"

I said—I don't know why, except that my head was still ringing—"Maybe Bob can take my place. He's been eying you ever since you got here."

She laughed loudly enough that I glanced nervously at the windows. "Oh Howard, you really don't know? Thank God he's not so squeamish."

We were still together often, the four of us, dinner maybe once a week and a couple of evenings at the bar. I was conscious now of Marty using me, a mischievous glint in her eyes, snuggling against me or kissing me too long, as much to be seen by Bob as by Danny, I thought. On weekends Bob left us at the bar around midnight, winking and saying something about "meeting me Luna associate, y'know." I went to the trouble—once—to note that Marty had indeed disappeared from the veranda, and to confirm that Bob's Land Cruiser was parked as usual by his duplex; then I checked no more. I called myself a snoop for doing this, but when I thought about it—plenty of time to think when the big engines on the dredge were running properly—it seemed like the way you glance out the window to see if the children are still playing in the yard. I regretted betraying Danny; I was glad I had stopped. Now I was part of Marty and Bob's duplicity; if Danny had suddenly decided to go to Bob's duplex on one of those weekend nights, I would have sidetracked him, sure that I was doing it for all of us. I suppose I was trying to make the best of things, just as in other ways. Your wife and family are halfway around the world, but the money's good, it gives you what you think you want, so you live two months with your family and enjoy those things, and talk about when you'll have made enough to stop; the other ten you might as well be in another galaxy or another century, or dead.

In late May when the rains were coming steadily, the gossips of Harbourworks must have decided, if they had known, that I was no longer involved with Marty, for I began to hear bits of news about her and Bob—how sometimes they went to the Ransoms' house instead of his duplex; how, on a Saturday while Danny and I hunted down beef for the Barnsdalls' party, Marty dismissed Akpan and spent the morning behind closed doors with Bob; how, when Bob was called to Port Harcourt because of an emergency with a crane there, Marty went with him to go shopping, and the emergency proved so complicated they spent two nights together in a guest house—not, as Marty had told Danny, in separate bedrooms at the Allans', who had been transferred to Port Harcourt.

Bob was called back to Port Harcourt almost immediately, and this time he stayed a week alone. When he returned, he showed up late Friday night at the Stevensons' party. Ufot, Bob's steward, had gone off to his village with the keys to the duplex, so Danny invited Bob to put up with them for the night. I went to lunch at the Ransoms' on Saturday—Bob wasn't there—and landed in the middle of the unpleasantness.

"Well, guess what?" Danny said as soon as Akpan had served fried plantains and a dark, crayfish-flavored soup.

"Danny, shut up," Marty said.

"I woke up early this morning and thought, 'Danny, there's something unusual here. I wonder what it is?'"

"Shut up, Danny." Marty's voice rose.

"I looked around, and then I said, 'I know what it is, Danny. Your wife isn't in bed with you.'"

"Please shut up."

I pushed my chair away from the table. "Maybe I ought to—"

Danny waved me back. "There I was. No wife. So I got out of bed and walked down the hall, and would you believe it? My wife was in bed with my friend Bob."

"We weren't doing anything," Marty muttered.

"Can you beat that? Right down the hall."

"We weren't doing anything. We were just talking."

I stood up. "I'll go on."

Again Danny waved me back. "Okay, I'm sorry. I'll shut it up now." Then he laughed, and his brows leaped. "But can you imagine the look on Danny's face."

"It was *you*, Danny." Marty turned to me, her mouth twisted. "Tell him, Howard. He thinks he's talking about someone else."

Harbourworks had the story quickly, for Danny was not quiet about it. To everyone's amazement, and relief, however—the compound was too small for feuds—Danny and Bob smoothed over the rift the same evening, and, when Ufot didn't return that night, Bob again stayed with them.

"Marty was telling him the God's truth," Bob said as the boat took us out to the dredge Monday morning. "She went to the loo. She saw I was awake, so she just came in to talk. Danny shouted a bit when he saw us, so I left. That afternoon I went back and told him that's all there was to it and apologized. So it's all patched up."

I said, "But that's not all there is to it."

Bob shook his head and put his hand down in the boat's spray. "That's another story, isn't it?"

Harry McIvor hunched his big shoulders over to light his pipe in the wind. When he straightened up he suggested, "Maybe Danny thinks anybody dense enough to dive in the shallow end of a swimming pool wouldn't know what to do with his wife."

Gabe Barnsdall said, "We don't want to believe what we don't want to believe."

At any rate, Bob was called to Port Harcourt again—thanks, rumor said, to Harry's maneuvering—and he spent the rest of June there.

All the wives and many of the men began to go on home leave in July, when the rains came incessantly. Harry had offered Danny a bonus to stay on straight through the rainy season, when electrical problems were the worst, and Danny had accepted. I was staying back too as part of a skeleton crew to keep the dredge going. In mid-July Marty, with several other Harbourworks wives, boarded a plane for Douala. From there she was to fly to the States and Philadelphia. The next day Bob also left, headed, he told us, "for Dublin and a barrel o' fresh Guinness."

VI

The weekend house parties stopped, and much of Harbourworks became a ghost town. Most of the servants had gone to their villages, so their quarters were empty too. All of us who stayed worked longer hours, and in the evenings we dragged into the Harbourworks bar tired and quiet. For the first week we were happy to leave the bar and the barman, Okpara, who was sullen because he was among the unlucky few required to stay on, at an early hour. On the following Friday night, however, I decided to visit the Luna, and Danny asked to tag along.

Danny and I shared a bottle of beer on the way into Georgetown. As Paul, my driver, slowed to pass through Ekpo Abasi, I offered to point out the "safe" women at the Luna to Danny. "You understand there is always a risk," I said.

"Right; I—what's that?" Danny pointed to something in the middle of the highway, a dark heap taking shape in the headlights.

"A body? Easy, Paul," I said.

Paul honked, then cried "Henh!" as the dark mound leaped up and separated into two boys in ragged shorts who ran off the highway. Other children laughed and shouted.

"Dese small boy play dis game in Ekpo Abasi," Paul said. He shook his head and clucked and muttered in Efik as the villagers moved stubbornly out of the way.

We left the village behind. A mile farther down the road I hid the beer bottle behind my leg as we came to the police checkpoint.

"They think if you've got something to drink you ought to share it," I said. Danny nodded, and we were silent as a sleepy man in a half-buttoned shirt, holding his M-1 rifle by the barrel and dragging the butt in the dust, peered in the windows and glanced at the Harbourworks insignia.

He pulled the log that served as a barricade aside and waved us on. His partner, who was asleep on a folding chair under a brush arbor, had not awakened.

When we reached town, Paul threaded the Land Cruiser through dark streets filled with encroaching market booths, taxis, bicycles, carts, men, women, and children with headloads, and darting motorbikes that roared past us on either side.

Danny pointed at one of the motorbikes. "Check his mirrors: one is for traffic, one for vanity. See? The right one's aimed at his face."

"I like their helmets," I said. "In Onitsha once I saw a fellow wearing a Dallas Cowboys helmet."

"Some of them are calabash shells, painted with metallic paint," Danny said. "My favorites are the fox-hunting caps. I'd like to meet the bloody Englishman who thought of selling fox-hunting caps to Nigerian motorbike riders."

"Sure you want to do this?" It embarrassed me to ask, yet as we neared the Luna I had a queerly strong feeling that I should not be taking Danny, that I was going to be in Dutch with Marty, Bob, and myself.

He laughed, "You're as married as I am, Howard." He was right, of course, but I didn't think of it that way; he and Marty were married, thoroughly married in my mind, in spite of me and Bob—maybe more so because of us. I was married when I was in the States.

The Luna was a large square room with a low, sagging ceiling that leaked in several places, lighted on one side with a string of Christmas lights, elsewhere with bare bulbs. Tables made of warping, rough-cut lumber crowded the room. A narrow strip of the dusty concrete floor was left at one end for dancing. The beer was warm, the glasses scratched and filmy. It arrived from an opening in one corner of the room after long delays. A loudspeaker over the dance area boomed Nigerian reggae and American rock. The prostitutes laughed and talked at a long table, their eyes on the entrance or the handful of men, Nigerians and expatriates, at the other tables. They were a dowdy lot, good-looking enough, but dressed in odds and ends of what I supposed they took to be European fashions—frumpish, badly-fitting dresses, shiny synthetic skirts, itchy-looking sweaters, high heels on which they limped and wobbled.

The women knew my habits and left me alone, but Danny was mobbed before he could sit down. While I lit a cigarette and leaned back to enjoy his discomfort, two of the women snapped at each other and tugged him toward the dance floor; another clung to his neck, whispering, and a fourth urged him to test the firmness of her breasts. Bob had put me through the same initiation four years earlier.

Finally Danny struggled back to the table. He sat down and pushed the whisperer off his lap, shouting, "I will say! I will say!"

Bassey had waited for me to spot her, and we completed our agreement for the night with smiles and nods across the room before she joined us.

I pointed out Felicity, Anna, and Nfim to Danny. "I'll call one or all of them over, if you like."

Danny watched them preen and smile. They knew that I was talking about them. He said, "I'll wait."

"New girl." Bassey pointed at a tall, large-boned woman with close-cropped hair sitting alone by the dance floor. She wore a lappa, the only one in the room, and when the light caught her face right I saw that she had tribal scars, ridges that rayed outward over her cheekbones. "Very bad bush girl."

"Why is she bad?" Danny asked. The woman had realized that Danny was looking at her. She stood up, watching him, loosened and retied her lappa over her breasts, and turned slowly, unsmiling, in a full circle. She had the straight, proud back that I associated with the haughty women who sometimes stepped out of the bush between Ekpene and Port Harcourt carrying enormous headloads—a log, a newly-cut stalk of bananas, a basket of bright orange palm oil nuts—and, without a glance at the speeding cars and lorries of the twentieth century, crossed the highway that cut through their world.

"She make fight," Bassey said.

Our beers came, and a Fanta for Bassey. She poured a bit of my beer in it. Then she pulled me to the dance floor, flashing her white smile. She knew I hated the speaker blasting overhead, but her making me dance was a wifely gesture, and we both liked that. While we were dancing, the woman in the lappa went to our table. She didn't sit down or fawn over Danny as the women usually did, but kept her distance. Danny stood up while they talked. She moved away when she saw Bassey and me returning.

I said to Danny, "We're about ready to leave. What's your pleasure?"

"I think I'll stay a while. I can get a taxi back." He was still watching the woman, who had gone to her table and turned to face him.

"This isn't the safest place in the world. You can get in a taxi here and never be seen again."

"I'll be all right."

I tried again. "Why don't you get Nfim or Felicity and come with us? If Bassey says that one is bad, you can bet she's bad."

Danny grinned. "Professional jealousy." As we left, the woman was moving back toward his table. Bassey was clucking her tongue in disapproval.

If Bassey liked going home with me, it was probably because she got what we both considered a fair price—we had bargained the first night three years ago and had not mentioned money since—as well as a good night's sleep, because all I wanted was to have sex and then go to sleep with her warmly against me. We were like an old married couple; often, instead of awakening her in the night for another go, I opened my eyes in the morning to see her standing naked at the dresser, pressing her clothes with the steward's iron.

After I took her home the next morning—not so early, since there were no wives to observe us—I checked up on Danny. A sleepy "Yeah?" answered my knock, so I shouted "Never mind." He didn't show up for work, but late that afternoon as I came in from the dredge I saw him behind his house among his yam mounds. The woman from the Luna was with him. Her lappa was tied at the waist, her breasts bared. She seemed to be showing him how to use a short-handled hoe, talking and gesturing, then chopping at the ground with it.

When I saw him again, it was at the door of my duplex around noon on Sunday, and his head and shirt were matted with dried blood.

"Jesus Christ."

He grinned, then grabbed the doorsill to keep from falling. "The bloody bitch nearly did me in."

Kumar washed and shaved the side of Danny's head to get at the long, deep cut, cleaned it, and announced that he would probably live. The woman—her name was Akon—had hit him with a beer bottle, Danny said, after they went back to the Luna Saturday evening and he got into a conversation with Bassey and Felicity. He wasn't sure how he had gotten home with the Land Cruiser intact, but he thought Bassey had helped. The irate women and the toughs who worked at the Luna had tried to surround her after she hit him, but he thought Akon had escaped. It wasn't even the first battle he'd seen her in, he said: Felicity, Nfim, and some of the other women had followed them outside as they left Friday night, challenging Akon's right to him, and, while he had held open the door of a taxi, urging her to get in, and the nervous driver kept edging the taxi away, Akon drove off the women with a barrage of rapidly thrown rocks.

"She had them running." Danny laughed, then groaned and held his newly-bandaged head. "She never missed."

"Maybe next time you'll listen," I said.

He nodded. "That's enough of Akon." She was, as Bassey had said, not only from the bush, but deep in the bush. She and Danny had talked at length, Danny said with a straight face, about slash-and-burn farming. She had gone to a village school for a short time, until a teacher had raped her, or attempted to.

A day or so later, Danny discovered he wasn't quite finished with Akon: she had left him with the clap, which Kumar and penicillin cured.

We worked through the dreariest of the rainy season, nights when the rain's hammering seemed to be on our brains instead of the tin roofs, days when, if the rain stopped for an hour, we cheered up, and if the sun broke through for ten minutes we stood around outside like released convicts. As always during the worst of the rains, I awoke in the night to think of mountains and snow, of mountain air so cold and dry your fingers ached and your lips cracked the first day. I promised myself a week in Colorado when I got home.

In late August Gabe Barnsdall got a letter from his wife, who had seen Betty Allan in Manchester, who had seen Marty and Bob together in Yaounde a full week after Marty left Harbourworks. Harry went to Port Harcourt for a few days and returned with the news that Bob had been transferred there permanently. And when the first Harbourworks wives came back, I went on home leave.

VII

My return to Austin began, Linda said, with "Howard-the-Bear marking his trees again." According to her, as soon as I recovered from jet lag I found my black bass trophy in the basement and rehung it; reclaimed my favorite chair and moved it around to the proper angle before the television; regained my half of the closets and drawers in the bedroom; pushed aside the yogurts, salads, and vegetables in the fridge to make way for steaks, breakfast sausage, ice cream, fresh milk, and all the other things we couldn't get in Harbourworks; and "bought back, pure and simple," Linda said, the affection of the girls, Melody and Cindy. I had learned not to bring home souvenirs, the carved warriors' heads and elephants darkened with shoe polish to look like ebony, the grotesque masks, the woven mats and tie-dye cloths for sale in Onwuchekwa Market. Melody and Cindy had each passed quickly through a year or so when these things made great show-and-tell, but now they wanted what could be bought in Austin's malls, and so did Linda. I came home with a carry-on bag, and that half-empty—other than my payroll records, not a roll of film, not even a postcard as evidence of a year on another continent.

Linda had taken a job as a receptionist in a doctor's office on Burnet Road the year before, explaining that she rattled around the house with the girls both in school. I had forgotten that until the alarm went off at six the morning after I got home.

When she came back to the bedroom with her coffee, she took off her robe and had begun to remove her gown before she realized I was awake, or maybe before she remembered I was there. She said a little shyly, "We're never sure when you're really coming, you know. I scheduled my vacation to start two weeks later than you said, just in case."

Still vibrating from the long flight up the coast of West Africa—Lagos, Accra, Abidjan, Monrovia, Dakar—and across the Atlantic, I thought that this was the best part of coming home, the honeymoonlike extra flush in the first-night bashfulness of our sex. I watched her dress, reflecting that most couples did not have the disadvantage of seeing each other age in yearly increments. She had been a pretty girl in Foraker, fairly tall, lanky, a cheerleader with flying brown hair. She had stuck with me, except for a month or so, even through the football-quitting nonsense. Her thirties and early forties had not been good to her. Her hair had grayed in streaks, her thighs and buttocks had thickened steadily, and her chin showed promise of doubling. Now I saw that lines I had noticed on her throat last time had deepened, the skin had loosened; the distinction between hip and waist was lessening, the soft crescent of flesh under her eyes drying up. Thinking that this lack of continuity to smooth over our aging was unfair to us, I wondered what bulging or bagging of flesh, warping of bones, loss of hair, or spotting of skin she saw in me.

We took the girls for a weekend in Dallas at Six Flags. I bought Linda a diamond bracelet for her birthday, which I had missed in July. It probably cost, I thought as the jeweler gift-wrapped it, more than my father had made in the best six months of his life. I spent two days with our tax accountant, another with a contractor to arrange for reroofing the house, and two helping Linda prepare for a party to repay, she said, "Everyone I owe for the last year." When we bought the house in 1974, it and a larger colonial-style were the only ones on twenty blocks of newly-curbed streets hidden in the live oaks northwest of Austin. I had wanted the colonial, but Linda pointed at the balustrade on the roof—we had been in New Bedford on our vacation—and shook her head, saying, "That looks like a widow's walk to me." So we bought the other one; now every lot had a house on it, the city extended for miles beyond us, and the money we had paid would not have made a down payment on the same house.

Our neighbors were young lawyers, architects, professors, engineers and executives in the new high-tech companies along Research Boulevard. On the morning of the party I asked Linda, "Do you think a diesel mechanic will be out of place?"

"Our BMW is as good as theirs, and the house too," she answered. "The main difference is, ours are paid for. They may ask you a lot about Africa."

"Not likely." I had learned years ago that no one back home wanted to hear a traveler's stories.

The talk was of easements, property taxes, and the Cowboys. One young professor wore cut-off jeans and ragged jogging shoes that looked as if they had been made that way. Our guests pretended to talk to you while they peered around for someone else. They were careful not to laugh too loud. Every time I lit a cigarette I braced for another story of how someone had quit or a comment about secondary inhalation.

Remembering the Harbourworks parties, the easy belly laughs, the good loud mix of accents—Irish, English, Texan, Indian, Italian, Polish, Scottish—Danny's lectures and Bob's banter, I felt a stab of homesickness. These people could have been in cellophane bags. As Linda moved about that warm September evening in Austin, more at ease than anyone else, I thought too of Marty and the half-dozen times we had gone to bed during the Harbourworks parties. I doubted it could ever happen among these uneasy, suspicious people. Then I laughed at how naive that was, knowing it could always happen. I wondered if Linda speculated about what I did over there, wondered without real curiosity if any of the smiling men with glasses in their hands meant more to her than an address and a wave in the street. Then I stopped: we had agreed years before without ever saying so not to speculate.

I settled into the easy life, supervising the reroofing of the house, fishing on the lakes—Travis, Buchanon, Marble Falls—mowing sometimes in the evening if it was cool enough, grilling steaks. Phil Mac Rettinger, who ran the dry cleaners in Foraker, joined me for three days on Lake Texoma. I prowled the bookstores around the university for paperbacks, new and used, to take back. During Linda's vacation we spent the week I had promised myself in the mountains of southwest Colorado and saw the first snows, another week in New Orleans. For a month and a half, I thought of Danny and Marty only when I remembered to feel guilty for not thinking of them. Once, at the Clarion in New Orleans, something in the gumbo Linda had ordered, the crayfish or the okra, reminded me of the steaming dishes Akpan brought to their dining table.

Then one morning after Linda had gone to work the telephone rang, and Marty's voice cut through all the longitudes between Austin and Harbourworks so abruptly that the receiver shook like a live thing in my hands.

"Howard, I've got a problem, kind of. In a way."

"Where are you?"

"Philadelphia. Howard, I'm pregnant."

"You—"

"It's Bob's."

"Wait a minute," I said. "Let me just get my bearings." I had put my breakfast dishes in the dishwasher and had been about to refill my cup from the glass pot under the coffee maker. The neighborhood had emptied for school and work; other than the growl from the expressway, the only sound came from birds singing in the live oaks. I tried to focus, to see Marty and Bob awakening amid their rumpled sheets in a hotel room in Yaounde, listening to venders outside with their carts filled with long loaves of fresh bread. Instead I saw Danny, whistling, bending over a circuit panel to sort out a forest of bristling wires.

"All right," I said. "So it's Bob's. You're sure."

"Yes."

"It would be simpler just to say it's Danny's."

"When we were home on leave once from the Peace Corps Danny had himself clipped."

"Clipped?"

"A lot of people were thinking like that, in those days," she said.

"Yes." I remembered reading about zero population growth in the news magazines when I was in Prudhoe Bay. "So . . . you must not be too far along."

Her voice quavered. "I'm not going to do that. I want it."

"Marty?"

"I've written Danny and told him. Howard, can I go with you when you go back? Please? I don't want to travel alone, and I don't want to meet him alone."

"He won't hurt you. You're not afraid of that, are you?"

"I don't know what he'll do."

"Did you tell him it was Bob's?"

"No."

"When did you write him?"

"Four—it's five weeks now."

"And you haven't heard from him?"

"No, but that doesn't mean anything."

Which was true; letters often took three weeks or more, either direction.

I said, "If we get there together he may think I'm the culprit. Everybody else knows you were with Bob in Yaounde, but Danny doesn't."

"Oh," Marty said. "Betty Allan saw us."

"Right. Did you know that Bob has been transferred to Port Harcourt?"

"No."

"You haven't kept in touch with him?"

"No."

"Harry McIvor engineered moving him. Do you want to live with Danny, or Bob?"

"Danny," she said quickly, then paused for a moment. "Bob and I didn't get along very well in Yaounde."

"What if Danny says no?"

"I don't know."

"Wouldn't you be better off staying here?"

"I want to go to Danny."

"You'd get better care here. It isn't just you to think about."

"Howard, I want to go."

Matching the flights took several phone calls; Marty had British Caledonia tickets and mine were Pan Am. She was staying with her mother, Mrs. Tapley, I learned when I called and Marty was out. Finally Marty got the Pan American flight.

Over the years, Linda and I had learned to dread the last few days before my departure, I think mostly because we were too embarrassed to admit that we were ready for it. Even the girls picked up on the impatience in the air, fighting nervously and spitefully without provocation, and scarcely speaking to me. I was ready to leave; I had had enough of mushy bread and meat, oversugared food, sappy commercials, and watery beer, of no-smoking signs and people who neither knew nor cared about anything beyond the county line. Linda too was ready: I could hear it in the edge of her voice, her chafing at my choice of restaurants or cereal or movies, at the space I took up in our—her—bed. The trophy bass would come down the weekend I left, the chairs around the television would shift. Just as I had been, I thought, a welcome break in the rhythm of her life, now she was ready to pick up that rhythm, and she needed me out of the way. So when, on our last night, she reached up to grasp the bulge over my hips on each side and pull me into her, saying, "Just when I get your love handles fattened out again you leave," we smiled, but we wasted little breath in talking about how much we would miss each other, or if the year would come when we stopped saying good-byes.

VIII

Marty and I met at JFK. We juggled our seat assignments to be together by a window on the left side, and that night as the 747 flew toward Dakar her head was once again on my arm. She did not look like a lover enmeshed in an international romance: her face was swollen and patchily flushed, her hair was unkempt, and she moved awkwardly, more like her time had come than a woman who, so far as I could see, was not showing. I was drinking scotch, but Marty stuck to juice; she had been sick every day, she said.

I said, "Still haven't heard from Danny?"

"No." She had complained about being cold as soon as we got on the plane and wrapped herself in a blanket, then asked for another after takeoff.

She said, "I got a telegram from Harry McIvor. He said I shouldn't come."

"When did you get it?"

She looked up at me through her small glasses. "The day before I called you."

"But here you are," I said.

"I didn't want you to have another reason to talk me out of it."

She sat up, keeping her eyes on me. "Harry said Danny was living with a native woman."

"Jesus!"

"Do you know anything about that, Howard?"

She watched me, frowning, her mouth pursed, as I told her about going to the Luna with Danny, and about his getting cracked over the head with a beer bottle. "I don't know if this is the same woman," I said.

"I was sure you were in on it," she said. "Thanks a hell of a lot, Howard."

I said lamely, "I tried to talk him out of it."

This time I knew she was going to slap me. I steadied my drink to keep from splashing us. Her hand popped loudly, to me, but the roar of the plane must have swallowed the sound. Other than a Nigerian in a white lace robe who grinned broadly, the passengers in the center seats didn't even glance at us.

"I'm sorry, Marty."

"Oh, shut up," she said.

She slept, curled up against me under her blankets. I drank slowly, feeling the sun rushing toward us behind the short night, feeling already the heat and damp of Harbourworks. A few rows ahead of us, a baby cried loudly and steadily. I thought about Marty and me, our times together, and recalled the small warm curve of her breast against my palm that first night. I thought of the small new life stirring in her and for a moment felt something like jealousy for Bob.

After an hour she sat up again.

"Bob doesn't know?" I asked.

"Someone at Harbourworks has probably told him. I haven't."

I said, "I've been thinking about when you and I were together last spring."

She smiled. "Our moments of intensity. They weren't very intense."

"Were you doing anything to protect yourself then?"

She kept smiling stubbornly. "Why should I? Were you?"

"I just assumed you were."

"You shouldn't assume. Or think. That's what I decided. Not to think."

"Bob and I were both sleeping with you."

"It didn't matter."

"I suppose that's what I was doing then—not thinking," I said. "If I had been, I would've asked you why you chose me, or Bob, of all people. The ones closest to Danny. I think you loved him."

"I do love him."

"And we loved him too. So why us?"

Marty didn't answer. We tried to sleep. The baby ahead of us stopped crying, but another on the far side began. It stopped while a small, thin woman in a sari carried it up the right aisle and down ours. When she sat down it began again. I awoke, sweating, as the sun's first redness swept over the gray cloud floor below us. Marty had put one of her blankets over me. Her head was on my chest. I had an erection, and her hand was over it, just over it protectively.

When I groaned and stretched, she turned her head and kissed me, her breath stale.

I put my hand on her shoulder and trailed it down her back and under her arm to her breast. I had been wrong, I realized: she was fuller.

"Easy," she said. "I'm tender."

"Sorry."

She rubbed her cheek against my hardness. "I could relieve you. For friendship's sake."

"Wouldn't you get sick?"

She giggled and sat up. "Yes. Oh, yes, I certainly would."

The sun rose and sank in the jet-shortened day. In the second, longer night, the plane leapfrogged from airport to airport down the west coast of Africa toward the equator. The in-transit waiting room in each airport was smaller, hotter, and mustier, each stop longer and more unreasonable.

While we waited in Monrovia, where the in-transit room's smell reminded me of the henhouse on my grandfather's farm in deep summer, Marty said, "I can answer your question. I never thought of sleeping with anyone else. I made love with you and Bob because you had the most of Danny. I was just trying to get it back. Does that make sense?"

Out on the tarmac a man was driving a tractor hitched to a trailer piled with baggage in tight, endless figure eights.

"Does that make sense?" she asked again. I nodded, and we stood at the window holding hands, watching the man on the tractor.

At midmorning we reached the suffocation of the Lagos airport and the herding and bullying of its immigration rooms. Caught in the press of leering, nudging touts, Marty fainted once. That cost us another hour, but finally we got through the lines, took a taxi to the domestic terminal, and caught our flight eastward. Harry and Gwen McIvor met us on the tarmac, shaking their heads.

"You shouldn't have come, Love," Harry said after he had kissed Marty. "Danny's gone off a bit, I believe."

"It's scandalous," Gwen said.

When Harry had gone over to tell Danny that Marty might be arriving, Danny and "that bloody tattooed bush woman"—Akon, it was—had responded by piling Marty's clothing out on the drive, except that the woman took a fancy to Marty's heavy silver dress. They had a tiff on the spot that ended with the bush woman throwing shoes, plates, and an iron at Danny. She had turned Akpan out, Gwen said, and Harry told me out of Marty's hearing that Danny had gone back to Kumar with "a dose of what she gave him before."

"The two of them work in that garden more naked than not," Gwen sniffed.

Marty was to stay with them, they said, until, they hoped, Danny came to his senses. Harry made it clear that I was to persuade Danny to do that. "If you can wean him away from that savage bitch long enough. He's lucky he's doing his job well as ever, and lucky he's blooming good at it. Otherwise I'd send him off to the bush to starve with her."

My chance to talk to Danny didn't come soon, however; at work he refused to talk at all, and at his house he turned me away politely enough, but firmly, or I was met by the bush woman, who said "Go now!" and closed the door. On the third day after our arrival Marty went over herself, against the McIvors' advice, and caused a scene that ended with her weeping as she left, the bush woman mocking her from the porch.

Two days later Marty caught a ride to Port Harcourt with Harry, was met by Bob, Harry said, "With open arms, by God," and stayed there. I gave up on Danny then, and it was a week later, when he came into the Harbourworks bar one evening alone, before we spoke. He made as if to turn around when he saw me—I was the only one there—then shrugged and came to sit by me.

"She let you out for bowling night?" I asked.

"Akon went to her village today, if that's who you mean."

"I brought back a bag full of books," I said. "One by Joseph Heller you might like. *Something Happened.*"

"I've read it."

We drank silently. Gabe and Harry came in, looked at us in surprise, and took another table. A few other men drifted in. I stood Danny a round, then he bought. The scar the bottle had left was a dark, erratic line under his hair, like a river on a map.

Gabe and Harry drank up and left. Danny said, "Know what Marty said when we were watching the van sink? She said, 'There go our lives.'"

"What did you say?"

"That it was just things. A van full of things."

"You were right," I said.

"I was wrong. All we were was in it. Not much at that."

We were silent again. I offered to buy another round, but Danny shook his head and drained his glass.

I said, "Why the bush woman? Why—"

"Does it offend your racist senses?" he asked. "I forget you're Southern."

"It doesn't offend me. I just think you're making yourself as unhappy as anybody else. You can't even talk to her."

"We find plenty to talk about. She's teaching me Efik and I'm teaching her English. She's learning much faster than I am."

"She's liable to kill you."

He turned toward me. "What's bothering you is that I've moved up a level in human relationships. She may kill me, but she'll do it face to face. I won't have to wait three months to find out it's been done."

"Danny—"

"Is Marty still here?" he asked.

"She stayed a few days, hoping you would change your mind. Then she went to Port Harcourt."

"Is she with Bob?"

"Yes."

"But she came back with you," he said, watching me.

"Yes."

He ran a scale on the glass with his fingers, like a galloping horse. "Is it yours?"

"No."

"Bob's?"

"Yes. She says it is." I turned my glass slowly in its circle of wetness, and then said what I'd known I would say to him in some form since that first night when Marty stepped on my porch. "It could have been mine, back in March or April. Not since then."

His fingers stopped, and his eyebrows arched several times. He nodded. "I thought so."

"Danny, she wants to come back to you. She says she loves you, and I think you two need to be together."

He stood up. His mouth twisted, and I thought he was going to hit me with the glass, but he set it down. He made no effort to brush the tears from his face. He said, "Fuck you, Howard, and fuck what you think. And fuck all good friends like you everywhere."

IX

A part of me would like to say that I moped with my guilt after Danny told me off, but I suppose few people are good enough to do that, if it's good. It is true that I asked for a transfer to Port Harcourt, but I changed my mind before Harry did anything about it; I thought that being around Bob might make me feel worse than staying in Harbourworks. What I did was go about my work as usual; I drank a Champion or two most evenings in the Harbourworks bar, I worked through my bag of books with, probably, as much enjoyment as ever; I wangled dinner invitations at the married couples' houses, and two or three times a month I called Paul, my driver, went to the Luna, and brought Bassey or one of the other girls back to my duplex.

Danny and I spoke when it would have been awkward not to, but we had no more beers together at the bar, and he did not come to the weekend parties. The garden behind his house became a forest of corn, pawpaw trees, bananas, pineapples, and climbing vines. Sometimes we saw him and the bush woman working there together, naked to the waist, wielding matchets or short-handled hoes. Letters came to Danny from Port Harcourt once or twice a week, all of which Gwen McIvor, who posted the mail, said Danny "dropped straight in the dustbin, more's the pity." Akpan, whom Danny had apologized to, according to gossip that passed from the stewards to their mistresses, was assigned to a new couple, a Dutch engineer and his wife.

Danny lived in apparent peace with Akon for a month. I saw them harvesting their yams one Saturday, Akon angrily answering catcalls from their audience outside the fence. The following Monday morning Harry sent Danny upriver to do some repair work at a relay station. When he returned the next afternoon two small yellow taxis were parked in front of his house. Nearly a dozen sailors were leaning against the fenders of the taxis, smoking and talking. Akon was taking on the crew of the Spanish trawler two at a time.

There was no fight, according to Harry, who had approved Danny's calling the security guards when the sailors balked at leaving; Akon complained that she had earned more money as a whore than Danny gave her, and said she was making up her losses.

"Danny found that a most reasonable explanation," Harry said. But a few days later he was back at Kumar's again, and with Akon in tow.

Christmas came and passed with no fanfare. It's hard to get in the mood in the middle of the dry season, when the heat and mosquitoes are the most unbearable. Those who could flew home. I had left presents for Linda and the girls in November. Their Christmas cards arrived the day before New Year's.

On New Year's Day Danny and Akon worked in their garden late in the evening, shaping new yam mounds. That week Harry came back from Port Harcourt with the news that Marty had gone home. "Bob was very sad they couldn't make it go," Harry said. "He was ready to pay for her air ticket himself, but I said Harbourworks could do that. Proper large she is now."

During a Friday night party in mid-January, Harry caught me as I was leaving to drive into town. One of the watchnights was with him.

"Danny's having a row with the bush woman," Harry said. "Let's have a look."

The watchnight ran to get help from the gate. He returned with two more guards carrying nightsticks as we walked toward Danny's lane.

The house was quiet, lights on in all the rooms, but we couldn't see anyone. "Danny!" Harry called. We waited on the front walk, listening. Nothing. But as we started for the porch, we heard something, or someone, behind the house.

"Use your torches," Harry told the guards. We walked cautiously around the house. The sounds grew louder, blows and angry, panting cries, and then the guards caught the woman in their lights. She was tearing apart the new yam mounds with her matchet and her bare hands. The rest of the garden had been flattened: the pawpaw trees and bananas were down, their green and ripe fruit slashed open, and the pineapples too. The vines had been chopped at their roots. The drying rack Danny had built for the yams was wrecked, and every yam had been cut into thick white slices.

She spun and came at us in a crouch, shouting in Efik, swinging the long blade of the matchet in flat, quick arcs before her. We fell back, the guards raising their clubs but moving aside too. As she passed us she whirled and backed around the corner of the house, still swinging the matchet. She went into the street, watching us, and headed for the gate without a glance at the house. The guards followed her at a safe distance, shouting and brandishing their clubs. I never saw her again.

Nothing in the house was intact. The coils of the fridge had been slashed, the food dumped and scattered on the floor. Gas hissed from the coupling to the cooker. Smashed plates, beer bottles, saucepans with holes in their sides, shredded cushions from the chairs, and ripped curtains covered the floors. Legs had been hacked from the chairs and tables.

"Get Dr. Kumar," Gabe told the watchnight.

The bathroom door was closed and locked. "Danny!" I called. "It's Howard."

We heard movement, and then Danny said, "Here."

"Can you open the door?" I asked.

When Danny didn't answer, Harry said, "All right. Watch yourself; we'll break it in."

The upper half of the heavy door had been furiously hacked and chopped, but it had held long enough for the woman to give up and turn her rage on the house and garden. Harry and I set our shoulders against the door, and the lock gave on our second try. Danny was sprawled on the floor in a smeared pool of blood. His nose was smashed to one side, one eye blackened and closed. When I lifted him his left arm hung loosely. Welts from the flat side of the matchet overlapped across his back, and another on his shoulder had left a thin line of blood. A long diagonal cut across his stomach was bleeding steadily.

He began to laugh hoarsely as I carried him to the clinic. "Howard. Do you know what that was all about?"

"Don't talk now, Danny."

"She thought something was wrong with her because she wasn't getting pregnant, so I told her about my vasectomy. Bad mistake. She was killing me to save me from myself."

"She damned near killed you, all right."

"From my perverted culture and its abominations. She'd never been sure I was a man, being white. Then she found out I wasn't even an animal."

"Danny, shut up."

"She could have finished me any time. She wanted to make it last."

Kumar patched, splinted, and sewed him up. In the morning we made a bed by taking out the rear seats of one of the Peugeots, and with Paul driving I took him to Murtala Hospital in Port Harcourt to have the bone fragments in his nose set. He slept all the way, even through the insanely rutted streets and stench of Aba, awakening only to complain about the cut across his stomach hurting.

I stayed with Danny in the hospital the first night, lying on the floor by his bed. In the morning the doctors discovered infection in the cut on his stomach and opened it up again.

At noon, needing sleep, I looked up Bob at the harbor. He took me to his quarters, and I slept all afternoon. That evening he and I drank together at the bar in the compound.

"'Twasn't fated for Marty and me," Bob said; "though I liked her as well as any woman I ever knew. But Danny was always between us, even in Yaounde last year. Marty would see it in my eyes, and I in hers. We had wondrous set-tos till we came to the truth of it."

"That makes sense to me," I said.

"Before she left she told me, if it's a boy, she'd name him after Danny."

"How do you feel about that?" I asked.

"Honored. Now *that* makes no sense, I reckon."

"It makes sense."

Later that night when the barmen were trying to shoo us out, Bob put his hands on mine, big hands for a small man, and said, "Howard, I'll see him before he goes back to Harbourworks. He can break my neck if he chooses, but I'll do it. What do you think?"

I nodded. "He's in no condition to break your neck. Now's a good time."

Paul and I returned to Harbourworks the next morning after I checked on Danny. The doctors thought they had stopped the infection, he said. "They're going to reorganize my nose in a day or so, when they're sure."

X

Harry and I brought Danny back after two weeks, his arm in a sling and his nose protected by a plaster tent. The area around his eye was still dark, the eye bloodshot, but he said it was clearing up. He walked and turned slowly; the cut across his stomach was still sore.

"I saw Bob," he said that evening in the Harbourworks bar. We sat in a corner, avoiding the center table where he used to hold forth.

"How is he?"

He grinned. "We kissed and made up."

"That's good, Danny."

"What can you say when an Irishman is blubbering on your bed sheet? There I was with a broken arm and nose, and one eye. I couldn't protect myself."

I signaled Okpara for another round and said, "Good. Now, there's the matter of your wife."

His brows leaped, but he shook his head. "Don't start that. We're quits."

By early March he was rid of his casts. Except for being thinner and having a slight curve in his nose, he looked like his old self. He gave up his house and the ruin that had been his garden—for a week after the bush woman had razed it, knots of villagers gathered several times a day along the fence to point and laugh—and moved into the other half of my duplex. We returned to the center table in the bar. Danny's latest topic was OPEC, or rather the collapse of OPEC, which he predicted, and of course, along with its collapse the downfall of the "Harbourworks playpen," as he put it. He admitted that he hadn't read *Something Happened*, and we began exchanging books again, Danny bringing good novels by African writers like Ngugi and Soyinka and Achebe that he found in town.

The first heavy rains came in mid-April, and with them letters to Danny and me from Philadelphia. Marty had given birth to a girl, "healthy and happy and beautiful, and needing a father," she wrote to me. "I named her Danielle, after Danny. Please tell him, in case he's still not reading my letters. He would love her even more than I do."

But when I knocked on the door to Danny's duplex, he shouted, "I read the letter, and I'm not interested."

Danny took his home leave in June. He was going, he said, to Kenya and Tanzania, maybe Zaire, "And maybe to the States. We'll see."

I went home in July. We bought a van and vacationed in the Canadian Rockies and along the West Coast, failing to distract the girls from the stereo and their comic books until we reached Disneyland. Back in Austin, Linda returned to her job, and the girls started school in late August. I supervised the installation of a hot tub by the patio. Then, after I had collected enough paperbacks for the return trip and fished with Phil Mac Rettinger until I had grown bored, I began to think of Marty. I tried to call her one morning, but was told there was no listing. I had not kept her mother's number, but I remembered her name and took down all the Tapley numbers in the Philadelphia directory at the city library. I reached her on my fifth call. Marty was working, Mrs. Tapley said; she had a substitute teaching job. I could hear a baby crying.

Marty called back that night. She had been in touch with Danny's family in Ohio; he had come home unannounced in early August, stayed a week, then left for Africa again.

"I should get a divorce," she said. "Don't you think?"

"I don't know, Marty."

"Is he still living with that woman?"

"No. That's finished."

"I suppose he tore up my letter. What did he say when you told him about Danielle?"

"He read your letter," I said. "He wouldn't talk to me about it."

"Oh, Christ."

Linda had taken the call. When I hung up I realized she had been watching me and listening. She was sitting in the new Queen Anne chair, part of the living room suite I had given her for her birthday. Her hands were folded in her lap.

"Who was that?" she asked.

"Marty Ransom. I wrote to you about her and Danny." Actually, I hadn't mentioned them in over a year, and then only to say that Bob and I had gone to their house for dinner. I told her about Bob and Marty carefully, repeating the gossip about them being seen together in Yaounde. I said that when Marty had returned to Harbourworks pregnant, Danny had refused to live with her. I said nothing about the bush woman.

Linda stood up and moved around the room straightening pictures and covers on the arms of the chairs. She said, "You and I are about ninety percent strangers. I don't know who this is who called you. I suppose it's her number that was on the phone bill for fifty dollars' worth of calls after you left last year. I don't know why she would call you. I don't think I want to know."

I said, "I could stay here. Work in the service department down at Wild Jack's Ford, or the GMC place. Or start my own shop, like my dad's."

"Yes, you could."

"I'd make as much a year as I make every two months now. You might not get a van or hot tub every time you want it." Linda had wanted the van for the girls, and the hot tub as well. The van had a refrigerator, wet bar, television, deep swivel seats, and huge green bubbles of one-way glass on the sides and top. The walls and ceiling were upholstered in leather. They bristled with stereo speakers. The camouflage-pattern paint job was trimmed with thick slabs of chrome.

"You think you hit me where it hurts when you say that," she said; "I guess you're right. But you like these things too. There are two sides to you. You like them; you like to come home once a year and buy them and act like a big spender. The rest of the time I take care of the house, our children, and everything else here. The rest of the time you are the great adventurer. The world traveler. That's how you see yourself. The truth is you go over there and they take care of you and baby you, and you drink and talk with the others as if you were great adventurers, but you're not. You're probably safer there than you would be on the expressway right here."

I shrugged. "Maybe. Danny Ransom calls Harbourworks a playpen."

"If it is it's because it's not home. All of you think you can behave however you want and then walk off and leave it. But I don't care what he calls it. I don't know Danny Ransom, or Marty Ransom, and I'm not involved in their problems. You are, but I never will be. If I ever met him, I don't suppose I'd like him any more than I did your precious Bob—who, by the way, was the one who slapped me on the bottom at that party."

"So what are you saying?" I asked.

"I know you don't tell me much about what you do, probably with good reason. I don't know who you sleep with over there, but I suppose you sleep with someone."

"I can say the same about you here."

"Yes," she said. "You don't know. We don't know. Ten months out of the year we don't know. We don't even make guesses."

I held my hands up blankly. "Where does that leave us?"

"It leaves us where we are. You'll keep working in places like that till you're killed, or you get sick from something and have to come home, or even till you think you're too old to work. Or maybe you'll meet someone you want to spend more than two months a year with, or even ten months—"

"Or you will," I said.

"—Or I will, and that will be the end of our marriage."

On the flight back across the Atlantic, I bought half a dozen little bottles of scotch from the flight attendant, lined them up on my tray, and leaned back to mull over what we'd said. It was a funny thing, I thought, the way Linda had been so sensible and capable from the first time I'd gone out on a job, a pipeline in Wyoming, and then in Venezuela, and then Alaska. She had managed well the big checks I sent home, banking them, putting them in CD's, and spending nothing on herself, unlike the wives of some of the men. I had known men who went home unexpectedly to find their wives running around in Continentals with their lovers and their closets full of other men's clothing. And there was Bud Harper, the cowboy from Oklahoma I shared a room with in Prudhoe Bay, who drew a thermometer on the wall: ten thousand dollars, fifteen, twenty, right on up he painted the red line; one hundred twenty thousand cash was his goal, and the day he reached it he chucked the job and flew home to a little dump of a town in Oklahoma to buy his ranch—he had drawn it with crayons on the wall, ponds, creeks, and cross fences—and discovered his wife's brother had gambled away every cent in Las Vegas. Before another roommate could be assigned to me he was back, looking thirty years older, his knuckles skinned from beating up his wife and trying to beat up his brother-in-law, and his face bruised from the beating a deputy sheriff had given him.

Linda had been careful from the start, and that was the first reason I'd kept on going out, seeing how the money mounted up, how the savings and loan people straightened up and smiled when we walked in to ask about money market rates. The stewardess brought me another glass of ice. I emptied one of the bottles over the cubes, shaking my head. If Linda had spent that first check on a fur coat or even a new bedroom suite, I might have been running a garage piled high with greasy, worn-out engine parts in some town along the Red River.

The first reason, but not why I went out now. In our argument, neither Linda nor I had mentioned that I could have gone to work at Wild Jack's and drawn, in addition, more than that salary again every month from our CD's. We had reached the goal that years ago we'd said I was going after. Why did I go back? Maybe it had to do with singleness of purpose. We were digging a hole in a river in West Africa. Everyone knew that—the stewards who scrubbed our clothes in the bathtubs and ironed them to perfection, the watchnights, the villagers leaning against the fence, the beggar women from Chad at Mbopo Pier, even the whores who came to our beds in return for our expense money. Let the hole fill back up; we dug it out again, deeper and better. Maybe Linda had been right that night when she screamed in the street in Harbourworks: we were a little concentration, less than a dot on the map, of whites, or foreigners at least, in a vast nation of blacks, doing something we had convinced them they couldn't do. Maybe we were acting like God, or at least minor gods. Maybe that's why I kept coming back.

XI

Danny was still talking about OPEC. He had subscribed to the Manchester *Guardian* back in the spring. While he had been on leave the issues had piled up, several weeks' worth at a time, so he had plenty of ammunition. He was also bringing back from town the daily Nigerian papers, the *Chronicle* and *Statesman*, *West Africa Today*, and the international editions of *Time* and *Newsweek*.

"Saudi Arabia," he said our first night back in the Harbourworks bar. "That's where we're headed next. Drink up now. Drink your scotch, and your beer too. If they catch you drinking there they'll cut off your extremities."

"Why Saudi Arabia?" I asked.

"Or Siberia, or Oman. Maybe North Yemen. Papua New Guinea if we get out of oil altogether. Because OPEC is going to flood the world with oil and drop the price, and countries like Nigeria, which have been cheating on their quotas anyway, will go bust. Even cheating, Nigeria's going bust."

Which was true, if you could believe the *Guardian* and *Time*. The trouble was, Danny said, that not only did the country cheat, but everybody in the country cheated too. Example? The case of a bale of old currency, meant for a Central Bank of Nigeria incinerator, that found its way back into circulation.

"A bale; imagine it," he said. "A hay bale of money. That takes cooperative corruption."

Later that night I told him I had talked to Marty. "She's still living with her mother. She was doing some substitute teaching."

"Good. Give her something to do."

"She asked if I thought she should get a divorce. I said I didn't know."

"Of course she should," he said. "That's obvious."

"You're being foolish, Danny. You two were as compatible as a man and woman can be."

"Compatible? You're—"

"No matter what she did. You were. Still are."

Danny grinned. "Talk to Kumar, Howard. You've picked up one of those parasites that swim around in your skull knocking connections loose."

We said no more on that topic, although as we were leaving the bar a few nights later, Danny asked me, "Did Marty say what the baby looked like?"

I thought for a moment. "No, she didn't say anything about that."

Danny had reclaimed his place at the portable bar during the weekend parties and resumed his practice of taking over the bartending duties around midnight. He became the favorite once again of the women, thanks to his scavenging abilities. He found pressed ham, real Danish ham, for Maria Perini, and the rounds of genuine Camembert that Sheila Barnsdall served at a Sunday brunch got him back in her good graces.

I joined Danny at the bar too, dancing now and then with one of the wives, but mostly listening to him, and we reestablished, at least partly, our old habits.

At the Perinis' party in late September, as the flush on the milling faces grew brighter and the voice of the party louder, Harry McIvor and I leaned against the bar by Danny and sorted out old Harbourworks people from new. "Old" meant anyone who had been there before I went on home leave, even if we'd spoken only once; that was enough, that meant we'd buy each other a beer some weeknight or slap each other on the back in the bleary hours of the party, I'd dance with his wife, we might swear to meet and get drunk together in Liverpool, or Nairobi, or Austin.

The new faces would be old quickly, or gone. A pudgy, middle-aged accountant from Scotland stood rigidly against the wall, an empty glass held at his chest; he had been wandering around the compound for five days, pasty-faced, lost. He answered vaguely when spoken to.

"First time out of Edinburgh in his life," Harry said. "Why they sent him is a mystery. If he doesn't snap out of it in another week we'll pack him home, and he'll be forever grateful."

Another new one, a pretty American girl, was dancing with the Indigenous Director. She had long brown hair that reminded me of Linda's twenty-five years ago, and her bare breasts swung heavily beneath the open latticework of a red blouse. Her husband, a hydraulics man, looked on uneasily. She was getting drunk.

"Gwen reports she seldom arises before midafternoon," Harry said. "Sometimes she doesn't get up at all. A common symptom: can't face the dark continent. She'll be running home to Mummy soon enough."

Fewer than half the people in the Perinis' house had been there a year ago. That startled me: most had slipped off without even a good-bye—men I'd shared dozens of beers with, whose tables I'd sat at, whose shoulders I'd slapped and wives I'd hugged with affection. Something about the compound, I thought, this gathered dot of foreignness on the equator, the fence around it: here we were family, closer than neighbors in any town back home; gone, we were dead to each other, without tears. We never spoke of those who had left.

"Peasants we are," Danny was saying. "Remember that painting of Millet's? The *Gleaners*? Except for the dollars, we're no different from those strawpickers. We're the moneyed peasantry."

Harry and I watched the frowning hydraulics man talking with his young wife. She turned away to dance with Archibald Ekong again, doing a little bump and grind before she moved tightly against him.

Harry laughed. "The lady just told him, 'You want Africa? I'll give you Africa.'"

"See you later, Danny," I said. "I'm off to the Luna."

He waved without looking at me. "Peasants," he said. "The tastes and cravings of the peasantry. . . ."

Paul didn't answer when I called for him in quarters. Finally one of the stewards, wringing out a pair of pants as he emerged from the showers, said that Paul had been called home to his village because of a sick brother. Angered because he had not told me or gotten permission, and also because I suspected he was still in the compound or nearby, drunk, I looked for one of the other drivers—Inyang, Moses, Ime—but found none. Then I looked in the Land Cruiser; the keys were in it, so I took it myself, cramping the wheel to spin it around in the narrow lane and honking at the gate when the sleepy guard moved slowly to raise the barrier.

I hadn't seen Bassey since my return, although she had sent word twice with other Harbourworks regulars that she wanted to see "this big man Howard." I liked our easy friendship, no different, I supposed, than what she had with a dozen other expatriates. We could talk about a few things: she delighted in seeing photos of Melody and Cindy, and she often asked me to come to her village to photograph her children, a boy and a girl. She had been pregnant with the girl when I first met her. She went to see them once a month. Her sister kept them, she said, and she would send them to school with the money she was saving. I liked her, her white smile in my bedroom and sudden clear laughter, her brisk undressing and careful folding of her clothes, the good-humored way she offered her breasts, her strong rise to me; her demand, as part of her fee in the morning, for the steward's iron to press her clothes.

I flattened the accelerator of the Land Cruiser, and the tall white termite mounds along the highway flashed by like road markers. There were no cars or lorries, just a few men pushing dark bicycles loaded with bundles of firewood or bags of cassava. I slowed as I came into Ekpo Abasi. Kerosene lanterns glowed in the market booths on each side, flimsy lean-tos stocked with soap, tinned mackerel, and small packages of biscuits. Villagers stepped off the highway ahead of me. I had begun to speed up again when I saw a dark shape in the middle of the highway. I braked and honked. The shape leaped up and separated into two small boys racing off the highway to the left. I swerved away from them, gunned the engine, and heard a shout, whether mine, or the rider's behind the bright chromed mirrors on the handlebars of the motorbike loaded with stalks of bananas darting onto the highway, or someone else's, I do not know. As the motorbike skidded, I saw the man's face before my right front fender, framed by the green bananas, not yet showing surprise, slender and delicate under the bill of a gray fox-hunting cap. As if he were in quicksand, he went under the wheel. Then the Land Cruiser was sliding sideways on the highway, the metal of the smaller machine and perhaps the man too screaming beneath it and me.

Before it stopped I was clawing at the door. I grabbed a handle and wrenched at it, sobbed and swore when I realized it was the window crank, found the door latch, opened the door, and fell out on the pavement. Then

I was running, running past the frozen faces of the villagers who had heard the grinding metal but had not comprehended what had happened, running as I had never run before past the last of the lantern-lit stalls, running on the highway between the walls of forest and underbrush. In the silence, my footsteps thundered on the pavement, but the shrieking of the metal was still deafening in my ears. I strained to hear, and not to hear, the frenzied cries of the villagers as they took up their matchets to pursue me, and that imagined sound was deafening also. I saw again the man's face by the right fender of the Land Cruiser, his face under the fox-hunting cap, slender and fine, handsome, showing neither surprise nor fear, and saw it and the bananas sink into the rending metal. Harry McIvor's voice repeating how Billy Reneau had been found on the pavement in Ekpo Abasi—"The trunk of his body and three fingers, and no more"—struck a rhythm with my footsteps. *Maybe he's alive*, I thought too; *maybe he lived*. A termite hill loomed up near the pavement, tall, white, and menacing; I screamed and stumbled, and a man beyond the mound pushing a bicycle with a large bundle on it shouted, dropped the bicycle, and fell away from me. I ran on.

My breath tightened to a shrillness squeezing my chest, giving me no air. I stopped and bent over, my hands on my knees, but that was worse. I walked on, holding my sides. My clothes were drenched with sweat. My head had cleared of the night's booze, but not of fear. Somewhere ahead, I knew, was the police checkpoint; I would be safe there. I listened for sounds of the villagers behind me, heard nothing.

I ran again, more slowly, remembering that the highway dipped and curved sharply before the checkpoint, and that a petrol station—a few barrels with a hand pump under a brush arbor—was nearby also. My stomach throbbed and hurt as it had from too much running when I was a boy, and for a few steps I tried to believe I was a boy, running from some terror in a dream, wishing it were a dream. I passed another man pushing a bicycle and met two women with baskets balanced on their heads. One of them said "*Mbakara.*" I ran on.

My shoes slapped as I reached the downward side of the dip in the highway. I gasped in pain as it turned uphill and began to curve. A single lantern glowed at one corner of the arbor over the petrol barrels. When I saw the barricade at the checkpoint, the gray log reaching snakelike across the pavement, I ran faster and tried to shout, but I could only cough and wheeze, and cry too. The policemen stirred on their chairs at the strange sounds. They stretched and rubbed their eyes. They were motionless for an instant as they saw me coming out of the darkness. Then they shouted, stumbled over their chairs, and backed away, dragging their rifles. One dropped his rifle, fumbled for it, missed, and scrambled away toward the bush. The other worked at the bolt on his, uttering little shrieks of frustration. I fell in the dirt by their chairs and rolled on my back, unable to catch my breath. The man struggling with his rifle shouted again and again. I heard a footstep beside me, heard a voice say "*Mbakara*," and felt metal against my cheek. A shirtless man bent over me. He nudged me in the ribs with a bare foot, and then I felt the metal pulled away from my face, saw light glint on the rifle as the man spun it, saw the butt coming at me. The night thudded and flashed, and then nothing.

I awoke as I was being lifted and pushed into the back seat of a car. My hands were tied behind my back. The right side of my face ached, and insects swarmed on the wetness over my eye and cheekbone. It was still dark. Men pushed me upright and, talking excitedly, crowded in on either side, tangling with each others' rifles, piling on one another. One was shirtless, and another struggled to pull on his boots. A man in the front seat whose cap was on sideways seemed to be in charge. He shouted, "Go now!" The overloaded car lurched forward and died. Voices scolded the driver, and the car started again. It gathered speed, hitting the axles at each bump.

"I'm getting sick," I said.

Someone slapped me. The man with his cap on sideways reached over the seat and nudged me sharply under the ear with a short, smooth club. I bent over to vomit. They shouted. The club glanced off the side of my head. I cried out, and it landed solidly on the back of my head. Then there was nothing again.

When I awoke the second time, it was to the sound of my own groaning and of many men chuckling. I could not open my right eye, and when I touched the right side of my face it was puffy, the skin taut beneath thickly caked blood. Someone had propped me against a concrete block, and its corner had cut so deeply under my shoulder blade that I groaned again when I tried to move my arm. My mouth was cracked with dryness.

Fifty or sixty men, most of them barefoot and shirtless, were lying, squatting, or standing in a small shaded area. Almost all of them were watching me, grinning and murmuring "*Mbakara*." We were under a pole roof of corrugated metal. The sun, behind a thin haze, must have been directly overhead. A high wall of gray concrete blocks enclosed the shelter. Rusting barbed wire was strung on rods bent inward on top of the wall, and two men with rifles sat on a shaded platform outside and above the wall at the far end.

My hands were free. Mosquitoes, I saw, had feasted on my arms, and my feet and ankles. My shoes and socks were missing. My wallet, I knew before I checked, was gone, and my cigarettes too. I brushed flies away from my face, winced, and saw fresh blood on my hand.

"Water," I said.

"*Mbakara*, watah dah." A man squatting nearby pointed at a tub on the ground near the wall by the guards' platform. It was covered with a piece of metal roofing. I got up by degrees, getting my knees under me first and waiting for my dizziness to clear. While the men laughed, I crawled over to one of the poles, held on to it, and pulled myself up. The wall and the men swam before me. When they came into focus, I went to the tub, stopping every two or three steps. I nearly fell as I crossed a trench latrine. A tin cup hung by the handle on the edge of the tub. I raised the sheet of tin and filled the cup. The water was tepid and something, larvae of some kind, was swimming in it, but I drank, refilled the cup, and drank again. I paused, remembered all the warnings I had heard about the water, and drank another cup. I relieved myself in the overflowing trench—it led to a hole under the wall—and returned to my place under the shelter.

"Where are we?" I asked the man who had pointed to the water.

He laughed. "*Mbakara*, dis na jail."

XII

I was too sick from the clubbing the policemen had given me to think about what would happen. I knew Harry McIvor would get me out, and each time the guards tugged open the heavy door in the wall I thought it would be Harry, but they called out names I could not understand and took away other men. After we had been fed cassava and a thin pepper soup, two policemen came in for me as darkness fell and led me out of the walled enclosure into the narrow hallway of a squat building with openings into a dozen tiny rooms. They steadied me before a small, balding man who raised his glasses to look up at me, settled them on his nose and continued to study some papers on his desk, my driver's license and resident visa among them. There was a chair by the wall, but the guards pushed me back when I leaned toward it. An orange with the top sliced off was on one corner of the desk. I realized later that I should have been frightened, but I was not. All afternoon, dozing and awakening, I had seen the man on the motorbike in front of the fender of the Land Cruiser, seen him sinking out of sight, and each time I had thought, *Maybe he's alive; maybe the wheel missed him, and he's alive.* I must not, I knew, admit any fault; I remembered the two boys leaping up, remembered swerving, saw the motorbike going down. The man had come straight onto the highway without stopping; we would have collided whether I swerved or not: I thought this, but could not be sure.

The small man before me blurred, and I must have sagged, for the men shouted at me, shook my arms, and poked me erect.

"Please get me a doctor," I said.

The man at the desk removed his glasses. "You are a murderer."

"No!" My legs gave away, and the men struggled under my weight.

"You killed this youngman."

"The motorbike ran under my car. I had no chance to miss him."

"You ran from Ekpo Abasi because you were guilty."

"They killed an expatriate there."

"You attacked the policemen at the checkpoint because you were guilty."

"They killed an expatriate with their matchets in Ekpo Abasi four years ago. That's why I ran."

"Why did you attack the policemen?"

"I did not attack them. One of them hit me with his rifle. Please, I need a doctor. Your men have beaten me badly."

He shuffled the papers. "Where is your passport?"

"At Harbourworks. Have you notified Harbourworks?"

"We must have your passport."

"Harbourworks will give it to you."

"You have no passport. Perhaps you are a spy."

I said, "I have been at Harbourworks five years. The policemen at the checkpoint have seen me many times. You know I am not a spy."

He leaned back in his chair and sucked the orange, spitting seeds in the corner. It was dark outside. When he had flattened the orange, he tossed it in the corner, took a handkerchief from his pocket to wipe his hands, and smiled for the first time. He said, "Mr. Westfall, what do you have for me?"

"What do I have—? I don't understand."

He smiled again, and his voice took on a wheedling tone. "You are an engineer. You are paid handsomely. What do you have for me?"

"Harbourworks will pay you," I said. "You know this."

"Your crime is serious." He waved for the men to take me away. "Perhaps you will understand this tomorrow."

The man who had shown me the water tub watched me find my place under the shelter and lie down, then chuckled. "Dis Sergeant Umuaro want ahm kola. 'E say, 'Dis *mbakara* rich man. Now make I be rich man.'"

Some of the bites on my arms and legs, I realized that night, were from sand fleas, although the mosquitoes were thick too. A few men had bits of cloth or mats that they unrolled to sleep on, but most, like me, had nothing. I slapped steadily at the mosquitoes, to the amusement of the other prisoners. There was no question of sleep.

Time stopped. Men were pushed through the door during the night, some drunk, some crying. They milled about, then found places under the roof. I scratched and slapped until I had no more strength to do so. Near morning, I slept.

Around noon I began to shiver, and the diarrhea started. The other men joked at first as, again and again, I struggled over to the trench, squatted, and afterward tried to clean myself, but they lost interest. Once I thought I heard Harry shouting outside the wall, and I tried to call to him.

When the guards came for me in the evening, the man next to me said, "*Mbakara*, make you give dis Umuaro kola. You no give ahm, you die-o."

The guards scolded and complained as they dragged me into the building. My teeth were chattering so badly I had trouble talking.

"A doctor," I said.

The small man behind the desk looked at me for a moment, then stood up and spoke sharply to the guards. They pushed me into the chair by the wall.

"What do you have for me?" he asked.

"If I die, Harbourworks will have you sacked," I said. "You will go to jail yourself."

He spoke again, but I could not answer him. The guards took me back inside the wall. Of that night, I remember thinking clearly that diarrhea led to dehydration, and dehydration to death, so I crawled over to the tub of water, drank, and stayed there. I remember feeling someone going through my pockets, an exclamation of disgust, a bare foot with filelike calluses scraping hard across my face, the sound of spitting, and wetness on my neck. Later, over and over, I saw the man sinking to his death under the Land Cruiser. Stories came to me about how he had become the owner of the motorbike—he had been very bright, had been selected by a priest to attend school, had become a government worker, and thus could borrow money from the government to buy the bike; he was a clever vender, had begun by selling bananas in the street as a small boy, and in his teens had built his own stall along the highway; he had borrowed money from a wealthy relative to buy the motorbike and was paying for it by driving it as a taxi. Then one night an alien, a white man came down the highway in a heavy, square-framed Land Cruiser, the young man had driven onto the highway just as the ponderous vehicle swerved, and his story ended.

And even later, when I stopped shaking for a moment, I realized that I was no longer slapping at insects or scratching at my bites. The mosquitoes were draining my blood away peacefully, the sand fleas sprang back and forth into my hair from the dirt mound I had pushed up for a pillow, and I pressed against the packed ground like a lover, desiring its warmth more than I had ever desired a woman.

Harry came shortly after daybreak the next morning, and with him Kumar, who scolded and threatened the guards so ferociously in pidgin that they whimpered. Then the Indigenous Director came, shouting and waving his arms, and the small, balding man ran back and forth hysterically, once actually falling to his knees and raising his hands like a beggar.

Danny was with them too, saying, "Jesus Christ, look at you, look at you." He lifted my head onto the crook of his arm, Kumar snapping "Careful! Careful!"

"The bloody bastard," Danny said. "We were here yesterday and the day before, but he was holding out on us."

"We thought they'd done for you in Ekpo Abasi, me boy," Harry said.

Kumar and Danny wrapped me in blankets in the back of a Peugeot wagon. The spasms of new chills their warmth set off blended into a long, bumpy ride, gray and white forms moving and talking softly about me, needles, pans, and tubes, and then nothing until the steel bars at the foot of my bed and the windows of my room in Murtala Hospital came into focus one morning several days later.

Bob Mullin appeared that evening—he had sat with me every evening, he said. "But your conversation was gibberish. Not that it wasn't before, but worse yet." That was on Tuesday. By Friday afternoon, when Danny came, I was ready to return to Harbourworks.

"They've flushed twenty-six of the twenty-seven strains of internal parasites out of you," Danny said. "They're leaving one as a souvenir." He had come with Paul, who apologized again and again; he had nearly lost his job, Danny said.

While I stretched out in the rear seat of a Peugeot on the drive back to Harbourworks the next morning, Danny leaned over the front seat beside Paul and told me about the man on the motorbike. "He wasn't from Ekpo Abasi; that may explain why you're alive. He was from Ikot; it's a village not far from Akpan's."

"Did Akpan know him?"

"He knows of the family. They're farmers and traders. This one's name was Uya. He was on his way to Georgetown to sell bananas and buy stock for his market booth: matches, soap, that sort of thing. He had a wife and two children, another on the way."

"Did he die instantly?"

Danny nodded. "The wheel went over his head. The fox-hunting cap was useless."

After a few minutes I asked, "What about Harbourworks insurance? Will it help them?"

Danny looked out the rear window. "Harbourworks made sure the records show it wasn't your fault."

"I don't think it was."

"Whether it was yours or not. That means Uya's insurance would have to pay whatever was to be paid—and your injuries too, and the Land Cruiser damages, for that matter. But Uya didn't have insurance. They never do."

"So his family gets nothing," I said.

"Right."

We were driving through a swampy area where the road sank out of sight every two or three years and had to be built up again. On our right were enormous trees with gray, flanged trunks. Their tops towered over the dark forest line.

"And I'm clear," I said. "It's too easy."

Danny said, "You're almost clear. The Indigenous Director got your driver's license and work permit back, but Immigration wanted your passport, and someone up the line is holding it. Harry suspects Ekong isn't doing all he could to get it back."

"So I can't leave the country."

"You could. Harbourworks could put you on a supply ship going back to England. Harry says it's been done before. I could get you into Cameroun and to the U.S. Embassy in Yaounde, if it came to that. Or this may be nothing, just a stack of passports with yours in it that someone is too lazy to go through."

I slept until we came to a stretch of road where the pavement had washed away, leaving a washboard surface that shook the Peugeot fiercely. And then I slept again.

XIII

The Sunday after the accident had been my day to write Linda, so I was behind. Two letters were waiting for me at Harbourworks, full of the usual news of the girls' grades, of Cindy's soccer team and Melody's dancing lessons. Cindy now had braces instead of a retainer. On Sunday, two weeks late, I wrote to Linda, apologizing for the delay. I changed some of the details of the accident. I had it happening in the daytime, since I could think of no reason to give her for driving into Georgetown at night. I said I had spent a night in jail while the police decided whose fault it had been, that I had been cleared, and it was all over except that Immigration still had my passport. I told her about getting sick, probably from drinking bad water, and spending a few days in Kumar's clinic, instead of the hospital in Port Harcourt. I told her about the man who had died, Uya, and what Danny had said about his family.

The McIvors invited me to supper Sunday evening. Gwen and the other wives hovered about me so sympathetically that Harry muttered, "Bigod, I think he did it apurpose."

The hydraulics engineer and his young wife had gone home. "I believe he feared she was about to join the Indigenous Director's extended family," Harry said.

I went back to work, and for the next few weeks while the rainy season played out, I did not leave the compound except for one trip back to the hospital at Kumar's insistence. Danny brought flyers to the bar announcing jobs in North Yemen, Oman, Saudi Arabia, Papua New Guinea, and even Libya. There was no word from Immigration about my passport, although I twice heard Harry pounding his desk when Archibald Ekong dropped by. I got back on schedule writing to Linda.

Her reply to my letter telling about the accident came on a Wednesday in mid-November:

Dear Howard,

I'm sorry you have had an accident, and I'm sorry the poor man was killed. I am glad you are all right and were cleared of blame. I cannot imagine what it would be like to spend a night in a jail there. I am sorry about that too, and even more sorry I wasn't there to stand outside and beg them to let you go, or to go find a lawyer. Whatever I could have done to help you, or just let you know I cared. But I will tell you something, Howard. There have been times when you weren't here to help me or just be with me, either. Sometimes I've thought I could die right here, and it would be three weeks before you'd even know, and another week before you came home. Last winter I was sick in bed for five days. Just the flu, but I was really sick, with 102 temperature and vomiting. Melody and Cindy tried to help, but they're little girls. I don't remember if I even wrote to tell you about it. I do remember I hated you when I was lying there. For not being here. If I could have just called you, or you me, it would have helped.

I know you pretty well, in one way. No matter how bad it was in that jail, someday you will talk about it. And when you do, at least this is the way it seems to me, it will sound like you were glad you were there. And the worse it was, the happier you will be. I've heard you talk about Prudhoe Bay, the men doing dope and all that, and the fights in Wyoming and the knifing you saw in Venezuela, or wherever it was, and I've always thought you were happy you had seen those things. I've heard you talk about seeing those men executed over there, too. I don't understand this about you, but I believe you want things like this jail business to happen. When the girls and I were with you that time in Harbourworks, you didn't have any idea how utterly frightened and lost and miserable I was, how I simply ached in the bones with homesickness. I wanted to leave there more than anything I've ever wanted in my life, but you kept showing me monkey heads in the market or old bare-chested women or some awful smelling thing to eat, all those things that made me feel even worse or want to die, just die. Right there.

I don't know why I didn't divorce you after we got back. Maybe I was just numb. That would have been a good time to do it, when I was so mad at you for talking me into coming to that place.

Some things you're good about. You've always sent the money home. We live in a nice house and have good cars, and the girls get whatever they want. Even your letters—I'd never thought about it till the last three weeks, but when your letter didn't come when it was supposed to it was the first time I could remember in all the years you've worked away from home. So I thought what I said would happen had happened. What I said about our marriage breaking up. I used to think that if you made the first move it would be easier for me. But it doesn't really matter.

I've been involved with someone here for about two years. I met him for lunch almost every weekday when you were home last year. He came to the party we gave, and he talked to you for a while. He was wearing a light-blue Mexican shirt, but I don't suppose you remember him. This summer we even went to bed together while you were here. I don't know what his and my future is. He is separated, and says he will get a divorce if I do. If I decide to do that, I will take half of what we have, and no more. You have earned your share, and believe me, I have earned mine.

I don't know why I decided to tell you. I hadn't meant to when I started the letter. I don't know if it has anything to do with thinking if we can go without seeing each other ten months out of the year and be fairly happy, we can do it twelve, or forever. I don't know if ten months is really all that different from not seeing each other eight hours a day.

I know this, though. When I talked about how bad I felt in Harbour-works, he listened. When I was sick last winter, he came to the house to be with me every day. And I know this too, Howard: I've just been more honest with you than you ever have been with me.

Linda

An odd thing happened while I read and reread the last part of the letter, trying to remember someone in a blue Mexican shirt. Umuaro, the little police officer, appeared in a corner of my mind, sitting behind his desk and eating an orange while I begged for a doctor. That picture quickly faded out, and instead he was walking on his knees across the room to the Indigenous Director, his face tear-streaked, his hands raised, his precise English deteriorating into pidgin—"Sah, please! Oga! Make I say you—" He and I were sharers, I thought, beggars in our turn, and I felt a rush of sorrow for him. Whatever he had hoped to get from me, a few hundred naira maybe, seemed reasonable, and his wanting it surely did not warrant whatever disaster Archibald Ekong had brought upon him.

I went to the bar and stayed there, skipping supper, meaning to get drunk. But after my first beer and a shot that notion faded, and I ordered no more whisky. I drank the beer slowly, and when Danny came in later I was sober.

I told him about the letter.

"What are you going to do?" he asked.

"I don't know. It's still sinking in. Nothing, I suppose."

"You could go home."

"It's too late," I said. "She was bedding him even while I was home last summer."

Danny nodded without looking at me. "I know the feeling."

"Ah, Christ, Danny."

He frowned and said, "I guess that was unnecessary." Then he suddenly laughed. "Here's your logic: if she's sleeping with him, you're out. Why does it hold for you but not for me?"

"They're different women. She wants me out. Marty never thought like that about you." I called to Okpara for two more bottles.

"Meaning my wife—ex-wife by now, probably—was promiscuous. But your Southern belle screws only one man at a time. What do they call it? Serial monogamy. One-at-a-time faithfulness."

"Marty is not promiscuous," I said.

"You don't think so? I do."

We drank to be drinking then, raising our hands to signal Okpara or greet other Harbourworks men as they came in, and later as they left. In my mind, to bring myself to hurt and wallow in it or to anger and taste it, I tried to follow Linda and reconstruct how she and the man might have met, in the doctor's office maybe, how their first luncheon and touching might have been accidental, how timid or brazen she might have been undressing before him in a motel on the outskirts of Austin, how gratified or disappointed he might have felt at the sag of her breasts or breadth of her belly, how eagerly or uncertainly she might have caressed him or taken him in this way or that.

Danny rose to play the stereo, a scratchy Everly Brothers tape, and they sang of clowns in love and out. The tape finished. The ceiling fan over us, off balance, creaked and complained. And what I felt was just sorrow that I felt nothing else—no hurt, no anger. I thought of the girls too, thought with not much bitterness that I remembered them that way, "the girls," not separately. I tried to goad myself by imagining Linda, one day soon, saying, "Girls, this is your new father." That stirred nothing either; other than the gifts and buying sprees, my coming and going aroused as much interest in them as the mailman's, and, without much fuss, I had reconciled myself to that years ago.

Protesting that we had stayed far past closing time, Okpara brought Danny and me a last round, and we signed our bar tabs. We were quietly drunk.

"I want to go to that village," I said. "I want to meet Uya's wife. I'm going to apologize to her and give her some money. You said Akpan knows where Ikot is. He can take me there. He doesn't have to go into the place, just get me close."

Danny watched me, his eyebrows hopping. "I'll go in with you."

"No."

"If you ask Akpan, he'll come straight to me to see if I think he should do it. I'll tell him no unless I go with you. We need to talk to him about how dangerous it is, and how you should behave when we go there. We should talk to Archibald Ekong too."

I don't want to make more of my going—our going, Danny and I—to see Uya's widow than what it was. I understood it as a payment for my part in Uya's death, a real payment of money, and of something not to get rid of my guilt but to see it and feel it; and beyond that, something plainly selfish that had nothing to do with Uya, but was tangled up in the finality, the conclusion Linda and I had come to. She and I were even; I saw little difference in the damage caused by my dishonesty, as she called it, and that of her honesty, as she called it. I supposed reaching out to Uya's widow was a sort of diversion of that other unhappiness, a draining off of whatever I felt about what Linda and I had held together with home remittances and letters twice a month over the years.

Akpan flatly refused to help at first, but Danny persuaded him with a promise of forty naira.

"This is a foolishly dangerous and needless project," Archibald Ekong said when Danny and I cornered him at the next weekend party. "It is mere adventurism; you understand nothing of this; these are bush people who have nothing and want nothing. They have no need of your sympathy, and you may die in your attempt to give it to them. You imagine this widow and her children to be starving, as they might after such a catastrophe in a Western country. This cannot happen here, where the extended family takes care of all. I assure you with fullest confidence that they are healthy and, in time, will recover from their bereavement. They are in no need of your assistance."

I told him we had made up our minds to go. "What would be a reasonable sum of money to give her?" I asked.

"Fifty naira, not a kobo more; that is more than they have seen in their lifetimes," he snapped, and went back to the veranda.

Akpan learned that the widow had moved with her children back to her home village, Afim, about five miles from Ikot, to live with her mother. A friend of Akpan's had a brother who knew her mother, and through him Akpan got permission from the mother and the chief of the village for us to visit. I cleared my draw account with Harbourworks and put together all I had until my next paycheck, 800 naira. Danny found a stationery box in Onwuchekwa Market to take the cash in.

On the road to the village, Danny warned me, "Remember to give it to her with your right hand, and put the fingers of your left hand on your right forearm. Don't belittle what you give her—let her know that you are practically awed with the size of it. They don't buy false modesty here."

So on a Saturday afternoon in early December we were brought on a twisting, two-tracked dirt road to a village of about thirty huts hidden in coconut and oil palms. A crowd of villagers quickly surrounded us, grinning with excitement and murmuring "mbakara, mbakara." The tallest of the men were three or four inches shorter than Danny and I. Some of the toddlers cried in fright at our white faces.

Akpan spoke briefly to a shirtless, barefoot man in a lappa and frayed sport coat, then told us to shake hands with him.

"He is the chief," Akpan said.

The man led us through the crowd to a two-room mud hut. Crouching to pass through the short, narrow doorway, we stood with Akpan and the chief on the dirt floor and waited for our eyes to adjust to the cool darkness. Others started to push in too until the chief spoke sharply to them.

We saw a slight young woman, a girl really, hollow-cheeked and thin-armed, with two naked children crying and clinging to the skirt of the faded dress stretched over the bulge of her pregnancy. Beside her was a gray-haired woman in a colorless lappa knotted at her waist, not much taller than the girl but broad-shouldered and heavy. Between us and them in the tiny room was a motorbike with brightly chromed but bent mirror brackets on its handlebars, the wire wheels twisted and the tires flat, the bike propped up not by the smashed kickstand but by bamboo sticks set in the ground on each side.

Holding out his hand toward the girl, the chief spoke to Akpan. Akpan turned to me and said, "Sir. This young woman was the man Uya's wife. Her mother is there."

Akpan spoke to the women at length, pointing often at me and sweeping his arm in the direction of Harbourworks. I cringed at his tone, sure that he was lecturing about our importance and the generosity of our visit. The older woman looked back and forth from him to me, frowning, but as he went on she began to eye the box in my hands, and when he paused for breath, to answer approvingly, nodding and smiling. Her teeth were ground down almost to her gums. The girl did not lift her eyes while he spoke, or when her mother replied.

At last Akpan said, "Sir. Give the money to the young woman now." I held the box out to her, remembering Danny's instructions. When she did not move, the old woman snapped at her. She took it then without seeming to see it, her hand falling by her side.

"I'm very sorry," I said to her. "It was an accident. I am terribly sorry for my part in what happened." Akpan spoke to them rapidly, gesturing again at me. The old woman nodded, grinning, and took the box from her daughter.

As she opened it I looked at the motorbike and saw that the mirrors had been smashed out of their brackets. I remembered Danny laughing about motorbike mirrors, one for traffic and one for vanity. I tried to imagine the girl's husband, the children's father, the man Uya's face in the circle of rusting metal, the fine slender face under the fox-hunting cap, but saw nothing. I touched the seat and looked at the girl, her hands clasped under the swelling of her belly. She had not raised her eyes. Something gave way in me. "I'm sorry," I said to her again, but she remained still.

The old woman shouted and held up the wad of twenty-naira notes triumphantly. A murmur of excitement passed from the people pressed against the door to the crowd outside and grew louder. I began to weep. Alternately cackling and muttering sympathetically, the old woman shuffled around the motorbike to press her dry, empty breasts against me and embrace me. But the slight girl, her children clutching and crying unheeded at her skirt, did not move, did not raise her eyes. And while her mother fanned the sheaf of money, wept, burst into greedy laughter, and hugged me again, I knew that Archibald Ekong had been right, that my gesture was cruel and foolish and that the money, money enough to buy the village and everything in it down to the last yam pestle, money enough to shatter the girl's life again and make her the enemy of all who knew her, the money and the pair of white faces in the mud hut comforted the girl no more, were no more or less terrible and alien than the machine and the white man driving the machine that had come out of the night and made her husband dead.

XIV

I had left Linda's letter unanswered for three weeks, but the day after Danny and I went to Ikot I wrote to her, "I don't disagree with anything you said. I can't think of anything to criticize you for either. It didn't sound like you were calling for the white knight to come galloping home to reclaim what was his, so I won't. If I've learned anything over here, it's that the world doesn't need any more goddamned white knights." I stopped and reread her letter then, but nothing came to me to say about it, so I wrote another page and a half of the usual news about Harbourworks, who was going on leave for Christmas, what progress the project had made, which engines I'd been able to keep running and which were down because parts were months overdue from Southampton or Bremen or Amsterdam. And I mailed it.

Just before Christmas, I received a card from Marty with a photo of her holding a smiling, black-haired baby. "I've written to Danny too," Marty wrote, "but I suppose he won't answer. Please write to me and answer three questions: Is he still there? Is he still mixed up with that bush woman? If not, is he mixed up with anybody?"

"Yes; no, and no," I wrote. "But he's hardheaded as ever."

A card came from Linda and the girls a few days after Christmas with thanks for the gifts I'd left behind in September. There was a letter from Linda too, no different, so far as I could see, from those that had come every other week for years. Her letters began arriving on the usual schedule then, with news that Cindy had portrayed "Plaque" in a class play about dental care, Melody and then Cindy had come down with chicken pox, and Linda had gotten a $100-a-month raise. In her early February letter, Linda mentioned that "Gerald" had taken her and the girls to visit the capitol and then to lunch. Over the next two months, I learned that he was a real estate agent, selling lots and houses night and day as Austin leapfrogged outward in every direction. He had assured her, she said, that he could sell our house for $200,000 "within an hour"; his last name was Berkeley, and he was teaching her to play golf.

"Sounds like a decent chap," Bob Mullin shouted. "Much improved over her earlier model." It was early April, a Friday night, and raining. He had come for the weekend, and we were with Danny at our old places at the bar. The Stevensons were throwing the party.

"We learn from experience," Danny said.

"What I don't understand is, if she's got this wonderful new life, why she keeps writing," I said.

"Habit," Bob said. "Old dogs, and all that."

Danny shook his head scornfully. "Obvious: she's hedging her bets."

I told Bob, "She's never forgiven you for swatting her on the rear when she was here."

His face went blank. "Not me. Falsely accused."

Danny had settled on Papua New Guinea as the place to go when the bottom fell out of the oil market, and now Harry McIvor and Kumar agreed with him.

"Look at it," Danny said. He had brought a *National Geographic* map. "Australia's here. New Zealand here; Sydney's three hours from Port Moresby. Jobs there too, and country where you can't find a track made by men wearing shoes."

"Penal colonies," Harry said. "We transported our criminals down there for two hundred years."

"You populated every bloody place with your criminals." Danny put his arm around me. "Look at us."

Harry said, "There's a hint in every correspondence from London these days. The lords of international trade are deciding where we can next inflict our wondrous machines and expertise. They'll pack us out soon."

Danny raised his glass. "To the hole in the river, which will silt up, and all evidence of our existence here with it."

"Get your money out," Kumar advised. "Change your naira. Take whatever rate you can get, whatever currency you can get. Change it, and get it out of the country."

Bob said, "If you take all *your* money out the blinking country will collapse tonight."

In late April a note came from Linda: "Gerald has gone back to his wife. With no warning, nothing. We went to see *Passage to India* Tuesday night, on Thursday he stood me up for lunch. I got a letter from him the next day saying they were back together. I just can't think right now."

A week later, on a Thursday, a letter came from her with the usual news. In a postscript, she wrote, "I haven't heard any more from Gerald, so it must be permanent. I've been trying to figure out where this leaves me. I guess with a husband I see two months a year who doesn't care whether I'm faithful to him or not. Unless you have any objections."

On Friday Gwen McIvor and Sheila Barnsdall went in a Peugeot to the airport to pick up some air freight for Harry. When they returned, Marty and a toddler who said her name was Danielle were with them.

Gwen met us as we got off the boat from the dredge that evening. "What was there to do?" she asked. "She was there with the baby, and a darling bright little thing it is too. She came on a one-way ticket."

"Where is she?" Danny asked.

"At the Barnsdalls', for the moment."

"I don't want to see her."

"Splendid," Harry said to Danny. "What the hell do we do now? Are you dropping it in our laps and done with it?"

"Send her to Mullin; it's his kid." Danny looked at me. "Or turn her over to Howard. He was in on the act. He can take her in."

"Or I could take you apart," I said.

"For whatever good that would do." Danny stalked off toward his duplex.

I went straight to the Barnsdalls', but Sheila met me at the door with her finger over her lips. "Marty said the little one fussed all the way from New York. They're both asleep now."

Danny was at the Perinis' party that night, at the bar. I took a stool beside him and began talking to Nick Allan, who had been transferred back to Harbourworks. I danced with Betty Allan and returned to the bar. Kumar, who had seen his last patient at nine, joined me to complain about his endless working days. He was interrupted after a few minutes by a security guard who said a sick relative of Archibald Ekong's was waiting outside.

"Pack up," Harry said. "It's Papua New Guinea. Headquarters got the notification today. We'll phase out and be quits here within three months. The word is anyone in Harbourworks who wants a job in Papua New Guinea will have it."

Then Danny and I were alone, and he said, "Well?"

"Well, what?"

"Don't be bloody coy."

"She's sleeping. Sheila said the baby kept her awake all the way."

Danny smirked. "Sins of the mothers."

By the time I left—early—Danny was getting drunk. He had already joined the Perinis' steward behind the bar, and he was pacing his beer with shots of Dutch schnapps.

I went to the Barnsdalls' again in the morning. Their steward stopped me before I could ring the bell, whispering that Master and Madame were still asleep. I followed him to the veranda, saw a black-haired toddler in a diaper making a mess of a bowl of cereal on the floor, and then I was holding Marty tightly while she wept and kissed me, mussed my hair, tugged at my beard, and wept again.

She was much thinner, the wear of mothering and whatever else clear in her face and, when we sat down and the steward brought coffee, in the set of her shoulders. But she was still Marty, the life still in her eyes magnified behind her glasses, still in her quick smirk and movements beneath her robe and gown.

Marty took turns wiping away tears and crying. The child came over to protest the hugs her mother was giving the stranger, became interested in my beard, grinned crookedly, lost interest, and went back to her cereal.

I began, "Danny—"

"I saw him going to his duplex yesterday afternoon," she said. "I knew just by the way he was walking there wasn't any use then. That's when I decided to go to bed and start fresh today."

I nodded. "Last I saw of him at the Perinis', he was working on a high-class hangover."

"Maybe it will weaken his resistance," she said. "Let me dress. Will you go with me?"

"If you want me to, yes."

At the door I said, "You know I love you, Marty."

She hugged me tightly, burrowing her head into my chest. "Yes, I believe you do."

Danny was gone. At the quarters, Paul said Danny had told his driver they were going to Georgetown.

"We can wait," I said, and Marty agreed.

He was gone all day. The Barnsdalls invited me to supper, and while we were eating, Paul came to tell me that Danny's driver had returned. Danny had ordered him to drive into one narrow, often impassable street after another all day, sometimes getting out to wander through the mire of one of the markets. Finally, after darkness had fallen and the driver had complained bitterly, Danny had got out at the Luna Bar and sent the man home.

XV

It was early for the Luna. Danny was the only male customer. He had half a dozen green beer bottles on the table before him. The women, I gathered by the disgusted looks they gave him, had already tried their luck. I waved them away too. Bassey, whom I hadn't seen in nearly a year, came toward me confidently, but I shook my head.

"I've made up my mind what I'm going to do," I said as soon as I sat down.

"Good." Danny pushed one of the full bottles toward me. "Decisiveness is good."

I tipped up the warm bottle, took a long drink, and set it down. "I'm going to marry Marty."

Danny's brows arched and danced. "Good again," he said. "This shows concern and responsibility on your part."

"Thank you."

We drank silently. The Luna's sound system had not yet been turned up to full volume. The women were sitting at the long table by the dance floor, talking and laughing. They glanced at us occasionally to see if we had changed our minds.

"It shows cosmic order," Danny said. "Marty has divorced me. Your wife is divorcing you. Marty is free; you are free. You are both free to make a new alliance, and not be free."

"And live happily, and so on."

He nodded. "Ever after."

"Your information isn't correct," I said. "No one has divorced; no one will, unless you don't get back together with Marty. Marty hasn't divorced you. My wife's boyfriend ran out on her, and she and I are back to square one."

"So what's this about Marty?"

"I'm telling you what I'm going to do, if she's willing. I think she'll have me as a second choice, once she makes up her mind that you're too stupid to understand she's gone through a hell of a lot for you. A hell of a lot more misery than you have. You've humiliated her pretty thoroughly, you know. And she came back for more. Damned if I know why."

"I suppose finding out your wife is sleeping with your two best friends—not one, by god, but two!—isn't humiliating."

"So call it even." I remembered standing with Marty in the Monrovia airport, what she had said about getting some of Danny back from Bob and me. I told Danny about that, and then I said, "I don't think she ever felt she was being unfaithful to you."

"Don't insult my intelligence."

"I said *felt*. She knew what she was doing, sure. But it wasn't malicious. It was part of our friendship, the four of us."

Danny grinned broadly. I said, "All right, damn it, laugh. At least you've been together. She's gone places with you that I don't have the guts to go to myself."

Danny checked the beer bottles and discovered they were all empty. He called for more.

I had another idea. "Remember when you lost your van? She took that a hell of a lot harder than you did."

"She hit me," Danny said. He rubbed his shoulder.

I nodded. "I saw that. She talked once about the temporariness of our life here, how we don't keep in touch with our friends. Maybe she'd had too much of that—the losing—and the van set her off. Maybe the baby was her answer to it."

Danny grinned again and said, "Listen to the philosopher."

"I should stick to diesels, right?"

"Right." His brows jumped and bounced again, then pinched together.

He said, "This is a win-win situation for you. Either way you'll see yourself as a bloody martyr."

I tipped the bottle and drank without answering.

"Tell me something," he said. "Tell me the little girl doesn't look like Bob Mullin."

"Just like him. Hair coal-black, Irish blue eyes, very small. Her mouth's a little off-center, like Marty's. Otherwise, she's all Mullin."

Danny said, "You son of a bitch. You know I'd do anything to keep you from living happily ever after."

"Meaning you're going to do something intelligent for a change?"

"Just like her to come on a one-way ticket," he muttered. "How can you argue with that?"

I caught Bassey's eye and raised my head questioningly. She smiled and nodded.

"If they're still holding your passport when Harbourworks shuts down, I'll take you out through Cameroun," Danny said as we stood up. "I can have you in Mamfe by noon."

After I took Bassey home the next morning, I thought, I would write a letter to Linda, sympathizing with her for losing Gerald. Then I would tell her about Papua New Guinea. What had Danny said?—Sydney was three hours away. If Linda wouldn't come to the bush, maybe she'd come to Sydney. Or who knows? Maybe this tour would be enough, and I'd just go home.